God orders our stops
as well as our steps.

—An Amish Proverb

Sugarcreek Amish Mysteries

Blessings in Disguise
Where Hope Dwells
The Buggy before the Horse
A Season of Secrets
O Little Town of Sugarcreek
Off the Beaten Path
Peace Like a River
Simply Vanished
A Stitch in Time
Mason Jar Mayhem
When There's a Will

When THERE'S A Will

SUGARCREEK
Amish
MYSTERIES

ELIZABETH ADAMS

Guideposts

New York

Sugarcreek Amish Mysteries is a trademark of Guideposts.

Published by Guideposts Books & Inspirational Media
110 William Street
New York, NY 10038
Guideposts.org

Cover and interior design by Müllerhaus
Cover illustration by Bill Bruning, represented by Deborah Wolfe, LTD.
Typeset by Aptara, Inc.

Printed and bound in the United States of America
10 9 8 7 6 5

When THERE'S A Will

Chapter One

I am sure he will be here soon," Esther Miller said, rising up on her tiptoes to peer out the front window of the Swiss Miss. "He is not usually late."

Esther had been standing by that window for the past ten minutes, peering out, waiting for her brother Levi to arrive in his buggy. Esther was right. Levi was very faithful when ferrying his sister to and from her part-time job at the Swiss Miss, the gift shop Cheryl ran in Sugarcreek, Ohio. She couldn't remember him ever being late.

"I'm sure he just got confused by the timing," Cheryl said. Esther usually left by midafternoon, but the past few weeks she'd been picking up some extra hours since early summer was a very busy season around here. "Why don't I just give you a ride home?"

Cheryl had already cashed out the register, taken out the trash, locked up the back door, and was ready to shut off the lights. She hoped nothing bad had happened to Levi. Esther had already used the store's phone to call the phone shanty near the Miller house, but no one answered.

"I do not want to put you to any trouble," Esther said. She toyed with the string on her apron, which she often did when she was nervous.

"It's no trouble," Cheryl said. "I need to pick up some more of your mother's jam anyway." Naomi Miller had become one of Cheryl's closest friends since she'd moved to Sugarcreek, and she also made the delicious jam that Cheryl stocked in her shop. Besides, Cheryl would worry if she didn't know what had kept Levi. Out on the country roads around town, collisions between fast-moving cars and horse-drawn buggies were not uncommon and often had disastrous consequences. Cheryl wanted to make sure Levi was all right.

Esther nodded. "Thank you, Cheryl."

"Of course." She gestured for Esther to walk out the front door of the shop, and she shut off the lights and stepped out behind her. The evening was warm and the sky a gauzy light blue. The soft late-June breeze carried a hint of the sweet scent of summer roses. Evenings like this, Cheryl was pretty sure the little town of Sugarcreek was just about as close to heaven as you could get here on earth.

Cheryl settled in the driver's seat of her little Ford Focus, and a few minutes later she and Esther were passing out of the quaint downtown area of Sugarcreek, filled with shops and restaurants that appealed to Amish and English alike, into the glorious open farmland that made this the heart of Ohio Amish country. Cheryl would never grow tired of the sight of cornstalks planted in long, straight rows and sheaves of wheat rustling in the breeze. High, fluffy clouds scooted across the sky.

She looked over and saw Esther biting her thumbnail. It wasn't as if Levi could text his sister to let her know what was going on.

Still, if anything too terrible had happened, surely someone would have found a way to let her know.

Esther let out a breath—a literal sigh of relief—when Cheryl turned into the driveway of the Miller farm and saw that Levi's buggy was parked in its usual spot in front of the barn.

"See, I'm sure he just forgot," Cheryl said, but even as she said it, the words sounded hollow. Esther knew as well as she did that Levi would not forget. He was not the kind of man who took a commitment lightly. They both stepped out of the car and closed the doors, and the sound echoed in the quiet yard. Levi's dog, Rover, was sniffing around the fence by the entrance to the petting zoo the Millers ran. The barn door was open, and she could hear someone moving around inside, but otherwise the place was still.

"I hope so," Esther said.

Cheryl scanned the fields around the house as they crossed the yard. She didn't see anyone working out that way. They stepped past Naomi's carefully tended pots of zinnias and asters that lined the short walkway leading to the house. The middle porch step creaked as they climbed up. Esther pushed open the door, and Cheryl followed her inside and into the kitchen.

Naomi, her husband, Seth, and Levi were gathered around the rough-hewn wooden table, and they all looked up when Cheryl and Esther entered the room. Naomi's elder daughter Elizabeth was in the kitchen standing over the stove, stirring what smelled like the most divine soup ever.

"Esther." Levi's face drained of color. "Is it time for you to be done with work already?" He turned his head to look at the clock over the kitchen sink.

"It is past time. Cheryl had to give me a ride home." The hurt in her voice was evident.

"I am sorry. I did not realize." He turned to Cheryl. "Thank you."

Levi seemed confused and genuinely apologetic. Cheryl was glad for Esther, but she got a bad feeling in her stomach. Something was going on. These were some of the hardest-working people she knew. She'd never seen them just sitting around at this time of day.

"Yes, thank you, Cheryl," Naomi said, pushing herself to her feet. "You must forgive us. We did not mean to trouble you. We've had some bad news, and we are still trying to make sense of it. We all must have lost track of the time."

"Oh dear, is everything all right?"

Instead of answering her, Naomi said something to Esther in Pennsylvania Dutch, and Esther's eyes widened.

"*Wirklich?*" Esther then turned to Levi and asked something Cheryl didn't understand. The family spoke among themselves for a few moments. Cheryl felt like an intruder and wondered if she should just come back another time. She was about to excuse herself when Naomi turned to Cheryl again.

"I am sorry, Cheryl," she said. "We are being rude again."

"It's okay. I'll just see myself…"

"I was just about to go outside and get started on my chores," Levi said, pushing himself up. She always forgot how tall he was and how broad his shoulders were. "Would you come with me?"

Cheryl tried to ignore that thrill dashing through her. "Sure." She smiled at him, and he gave the slightest hint of a grin, and in his eyes she could see that he was pleased. Cheryl didn't look at Naomi. She knew her friend was worried about what seemed to be a growing attraction between her stepson and her English friend.

"I will explain what is going on," Levi said, and she nodded and followed him out the back door of the house and into the yard. With long strides, he crossed the dirt patch and went around the side of the house toward the barn. Cheryl tried her best to keep up, and Levi, realizing this, slowed his steps. As thrilled as she was with the opportunity to be alone with him, Cheryl knew it was somewhat unusual for an Amish man to go off with an English woman like this, and she realized the circumstances must be difficult indeed.

"My uncle Silas passed away very early this morning," Levi said. His footsteps crunched in the dirt. "He was my father's oldest brother."

"Oh no." So that explained all the long faces. A death in the family was a perfectly reasonable excuse for losing track of time. She thought she had met Silas at some family events she'd attended with Naomi, though she couldn't be sure. Amish men all had the same wardrobes and wore the same beards, and sometimes it was difficult to keep them all straight.

"Your father must be upset."

"Yes," Levi said. "He will miss his brother."

Cheryl was used to the stoic manner in which her Amish friends often reacted to bad news, so this simple answer didn't surprise her.

They had reached the barn, and as they stepped inside, Levi called out something in Pennsylvania Dutch. Voices Cheryl recognized called back. She turned and saw Levi's brothers, Caleb and Eli, at the far end of the barn. She waved and then followed Levi the other way, toward the stalls where the family's horses were kept. The air in the barn was cool and dusty and smelled of sweet hay.

"I had been saving up to buy a plot of land from my uncle," Levi said as he grabbed a pitchfork that was resting against the wall.

"Oh." Cheryl looked around at the tall, solid walls of the barn. She trailed her fingers along the soft muzzle of a yearling with a gorgeous reddish-brown coat. He sniffed her hand and then let her pet him. "I didn't realize. Why?"

Levi hoisted the pitchfork and dug the prongs into an open bin of hay. Little clouds of dust rose from the hay, and a clean, earthy scent filled the air.

"I plan to have my own farm someday," he said, hefting a load of hay from the bin. "When I get married, I would like to have my own land and my own house." He didn't look at her as he tossed the hay into the first stall. Was he thinking about marriage for any particular reason? Cheryl wondered. Or was this just the kind of thing Amish men did? She noticed that his cheeks had turned a light shade of pink, though she couldn't say whether this was from the exertion or from something else.

"You won't take over this farm?" Cheryl asked. Levi was the oldest of his father's six children, and Cheryl had just assumed he planned to take over the farm someday. She ran her hand down the horse's velvety neck, and then she moved on to the next stall, where her horse, Ranger, was kept. Levi had given her the horse for her birthday. She ran her fingers along his soft muzzle, and Ranger leaned into her hand.

Levi shook his head and hoisted another batch of hay on to his pitchfork. "In our culture, the farm always passes to the youngest son. So Eli will inherit this farm someday. I will need to buy land of my own." He dropped the hay into a bin inside the first stall. "My uncle Silas had no children, and he was planning to sell me a parcel of his land." The gray horse inside bent his neck and started chomping on the hay.

"So what does that mean, now that he's gone?" Cheryl asked. "Will you still get to buy the land?"

"My father is in charge of making sure my uncle's will is carried out," Levi said.

That made him the executor, Cheryl knew, but she was too thrown off to tell him that.

"Your uncle had a will?"

"Yes. Many Amish people have wills," Levi said. "If they do not, the government can decide how to distribute their things when they die." Another pitch, and hay landed in the next stall.

"I know that," Cheryl said. That was the point of a will, to make it clear how you wanted your assets distributed when you died so you didn't have to rely on the government to do so. "I just didn't realize...I mean..."

"You didn't think the Amish used wills?" Levi said. He straightened up and gave her a wry smile.

In truth, she'd never given any thought to whether Amish people wrote wills. But she did know that they avoided lawsuits, so she had naturally assumed they wouldn't. She needed to stop assuming things where Naomi and her family were concerned.

"In any case, my father has seen the will, and he told me today that Uncle Silas left the house and most of the land to his brother Emmon, but he left the parcel of land I had planned to buy to me."

"Levi, that's wonderful," Cheryl said and immediately hated herself for it. "I mean, it's not wonderful that your uncle passed away. What I meant was, it's wonderful that you will get your land and you won't even have to buy it now."

"Yes, it is very kind of him," Levi said. "I was very happy to hear it."

"And your dad knew this whole time? Why didn't he say something to you about the fact that you would inherit the land?"

"Why would he do that?" Levi shrugged. "If I had known I would inherit the land and didn't need to buy it, I would not have been motivated to save my money. It would not have helped things for me to know this."

Cheryl had to admit that might be true in her case, but she couldn't imagine Levi not working hard no matter what.

"Besides, no one knew Uncle Silas would pass away so soon," Levi said. "It was very sudden. A heart attack. He should have had many more years left. I would have bought it from him if he had lived long enough."

Cheryl could see his point. It probably had been for the best that Seth hadn't told Levi about being included in Silas's will.

"In any case, it might not matter because just this afternoon we got a call from Jessica Stockton."

Cheryl knew Jessica, a "Yoder Toter." She had a van and was often hired to drive Amish families around when they needed to go farther than their horse and buggies would allow.

"Why?"

"She said her husband works in the land development department at the county office over in New Philadelphia. He told her that someone came in this afternoon to see about buying the land that had belonged to Silas. He learned that Silas had passed away and thought the land would be available for sale. He did not know the man, but he recognized our name, and Jessica, who has driven our family many times, called here to make sure we knew."

Had word spread about Silas's death so quickly? But even if it had, what would have made him think the land would be available? Wouldn't he assume the land would pass to Silas's heirs? And why would Jessica bother to contact Silas's family about it?

"I hope he told him it was already spoken for." Cheryl had met Jeff Stockton. He was a straight shooter and wouldn't let this person waste their time sniffing around land that wasn't for sale.

"He did not know, but he did tell him it would be up to the will to say who got the house. But the man told him the land did not belong to Uncle Silas in the first place, so he could not leave it to anyone." Levi pitched more hay into a stall, and Cheryl noticed that his motions were getting stiffer as he talked.

"But that's crazy. Your uncle owned that land, right?"

"We thought so," Levi said. "But now the people at the county records office are saying they cannot find any record that he did."

"What do they mean, they can't find any record? Don't they keep records about this sort of thing?"

"They cannot find it." A load of hay missed the feed bin and fell to the floor.

"What? How is that possible?"

"I do not know." Levi hefted another load of hay and dropped it into Ranger's bin. The physical activity seemed to make him feel better, and he kept moving.

Cheryl puzzled this over. It didn't make any sense. If Silas had owned the land, there should be a record of it with the county. "Is there just no record of Silas owning it, or no record of the land at all?"

"I do not know."

Down at the far end of the barn, they heard the scrape of the milking stool across the floor and the sound of the metal bucket being set down.

"Well, then, where is your uncle's copy of the deed? You should be able to just show it and clear all of this up."

"That is the problem. We do not know where Uncle Silas's copy of the deed is. *Daed* and I went over to his house this evening to find it. That is why I missed picking up Esther," he said. Another forkful of hay came from the bin into the stall. "The deed for the house and the main piece of land is there, but there was nothing for the section of land he left to me."

"Where did he keep his important papers?"

"In his office. We searched everywhere. But we did not find the deed."

Cheryl thought for a moment. "What about mortgage statements? If he'd been paying a mortgage on the land, that would show he owned it, right?"

Levi set the pitchfork down and wiped his sleeve across his face. "Daed says he paid cash. Ten years ago the land wasn't worth nearly what it is today."

Cheryl let her fingers tangle up in Ranger's soft mane.

"So what will you do?" Cheryl asked.

"I do not know," Levi said. "If we do not find that deed, I will lose the land, I suppose."

It couldn't end like that. There had to be a way to fight this.

"You're not going to let that happen, are you?"

"I will try not to." He took in a deep breath and let it out slowly, and then he turned to her. "Actually, we were wondering if you might be able to help."

"Me?" Cheryl wasn't sure what to say. Of course she wanted to help him, but how could she be of any use?

"You know much more about legal matters than we do." His cheeks were still pink, and he picked up the pitchfork again, almost as if he needed something to do with his hands. "We do not understand all of these things. But you..." His voice trailed off. "You are good with this."

Cheryl was touched that he had asked, but she wasn't sure how he thought she might be able to help. She wasn't a lawyer, and she didn't know much about the legalities of buying and selling property. Still, of course she wanted to help however she could. He was probably right that she knew more than her Amish friends did. And she knew how much this land meant to him. She knew what a difference it would make in his future—in the future of his whole family...whoever that might be.

"Of course I'll help." Cheryl didn't know what it would entail, but she did know that she would do whatever it took to help Levi get that land.

CHAPTER TWO

First thing the next morning, Cheryl headed to the Tuscarawas County Recorder's Office in New Philadelphia, about a twenty-minute drive from Aunt Mitzi's house. She pulled up in front of the county's administrative office building, an Italianate building of warm yellow stone, just before nine, and she stepped inside the cool, quiet lobby at the same time as several men and women in suits carrying large mugs of coffee. She inquired at the front desk and was directed to the third floor, where Jeff Stockton's office was. She found his office easily, partway down a long hallway, and knocked gingerly on the half-open door. A nameplate on the door said Jeff Stockton, Land Development Director.

"Jeff?" Cheryl had met Jeff briefly after a Christmas service at Silo Church, but she wasn't sure if he'd remember her. He looked up and smiled.

"Hello. Cheryl, right?"

Cheryl nodded. "Exactly. Cheryl Cooper. We met at Silo Church."

"That's right. Jessica introduced us. You're friends with Naomi Miller, aren't you?" Jeff was solidly built, with wide shoulders and a round waist, and his graying brown hair was receding. His face was kind, and his voice was welcoming.

"That's right. I wasn't sure if you'd remember."

"It's hard to forget that hair," he said, grinning as he gestured for her to step in. It was a standard office, with a wooden desk and padded chairs. The walls looked yellowish in the fluorescent overhead lights. But Cheryl smiled when she noticed a line of Star Wars figurines along the bookshelf over the desk.

"Yeah, I guess that's true." Cheryl laughed and ran her fingers through her short, spiky red hair. "It's memorable, if nothing else."

"It's beautiful. My mother was a redhead, so I've got a soft spot for them. You're Mitzi's niece, right? You took over her shop when she went overseas?"

Cheryl nodded. "You do have a good memory."

"Trust me, it's the hair. How is everything going with the shop? My wife loves going in there."

"It's good. I love running it, and the shop has been busy, especially now as the weather has gotten warmer."

"That's good to hear." His shirt was stretched across his belly, gaping a bit between buttons, but it was nicely made and a beautiful shade of sky blue. "So what can I help you with?"

"I've got something of a strange question," Cheryl said as she lowered herself into one of the chairs.

"Is this about the land that Amish guy owned?"

Cheryl nodded.

"That was the craziest thing," Jeff said, shaking his head. "Out of nowhere an offer came in for this land, and we didn't know what was going on. We didn't even know the owner was deceased, let alone that the land was available for sale. Something seemed fishy, which is why I told Jessica so she could let her friends know. But when I checked with the records department, I was told there aren't any records of him ever owning the land."

He leaned forward and took a small handful of jelly beans from a dish on his desk and then held them out to her. Cheryl shook her head, and he shrugged and popped some into his mouth.

"A lot of people around here, they aren't always totally above board with things when it comes to the Amish, unfortunately," Jeff continued. "Because most of them don't have much of an education, a lot of people think they're not smart, which isn't true. And they have a reputation for not suing, which doesn't always work in their favor. But based on what I found digging around here yesterday, I can't say that anything is wrong about this case necessarily."

"I don't understand how the title is just not on file. How can that be possible?"

"It probably shouldn't be." He ate another jelly bean and then said, "My department manages the sale and development of land in the county. So when an offer for the land came in, I went and looked for the certificate of title in our database. That's standard, to see who actually owns the land and such. And it was really strange. There's just no entry for that plot of land."

"Is that unusual?"

"Only if the land isn't registered. A few years ago it wouldn't have been that unusual to have plots of land with no claim on them, but with the way prices have skyrocketed around here in recent years, it would be quite strange."

"Is there a paper copy of the title anywhere?"

"There is supposed to be," Jeff said, popping another jelly bean in his mouth. "But I asked the clerk, Carolyn, to search through the files, and it's just not there."

Could Levi's family be mistaken about Silas owning the land? She couldn't see how this made sense.

"Is there any record of prior ownership of the land?"

"None. There isn't even a record of that parcel."

"How is that possible?"

He used his finger to poke around in the candy dish and pulled out a red jelly bean. "I wish I knew what to tell you. Like I said, it's unusual. Either something strange is going on, or no one owned that land."

"But Silas Miller owned it."

"I believe you. These Amish, they're not likely to make something like that up." He popped the jelly bean into his mouth and leaned back in his desk chair. "Do you know where the copy of the title is?"

"They're looking for it," Cheryl answered.

"Do you know who he bought it from? It's possible they might have some records that would be helpful."

Cheryl shook her head. She'd have to find that out.

"Unfortunately, with no record of it in the county files, our hands are tied. Officially, right now, it looks like the land belongs to Tuscarawas County." He chewed the red jelly bean. "And, unfortunately, with an offer on the land already, I'm not sure how long I'll be able to hold off on the sale."

"You mean the county is going to accept the offer for the land?"

"I have urged caution and asked for time to make sure everything is in order, but I'm afraid it was a handsome offer, and we've got a budget shortfall for this year, and, well, my superiors are in favor of accepting it. I'm trying to stop it, but I fear I might not win this battle."

"But how could they do that? If there's some question of whose land it actually is, how could a sale go through?"

"That's my feeling as well." He picked up a pen that was lying on his desk and started turning it over in his hands. "But unfortunately, things seem to be moving pretty quickly and easily for him on this."

"How is that possible?"

He sat up straighter, looked out at the hallway, and then lowered his voice. "I don't know, but my guess is that the buyer knows some people pretty high up around here."

Cheryl understood now. "Oh dear."

"Like I said, I'm trying to do what I can to help because I hate to see the Amish being taken advantage of like this. But unfortunately, the way the system works is that what's in the county records is the primary evidence of ownership, so as things stand now, the onus really is on the family to prove that he had some claim to that land."

Cheryl took all this in, her heart sinking. There had to be some way to stop this.

"This offer. Can I ask who it came in from?"

"I'm not at liberty to say, I'm afraid," he said, shaking his head. He really did look frustrated that he couldn't tell her.

Well, there had to be some way to figure it out. Maybe he couldn't tell her the exact name, but she might be able to get him to tell her something. "Is it someone who wants to farm the land?" If so, it was probably someone Amish.

"No." He leaned forward, glancing out toward the hallway. There was no one around, so he went on. "It's not someone who wants to farm. It's someone who wants to develop the land."

"To develop it?" Cheryl thought about this. Back in Columbus, "development" meant someone was building high-end condos or a shopping center. But who would build something like that all the way out here? These back roads couldn't handle the traffic either of those options would bring. "Is it someone from Sugarcreek who wants to develop it?"

He glanced out at the hallway again and then back at her and said, "The party in question is from Canton."

Canton. Interesting. So a developer from the city was looking to get the land. Cheryl couldn't imagine why for the life of her. She thought for a minute and then asked something else that had been bothering her.

"How did the buyer know that the land wasn't registered to Silas Miller in the county's records?"

"That is a very good question." He looked at her, tapping his pen on the desk. "And one that I am pushing for the county to look into before the sale goes through. But we'll see what the powers that be decide."

"*Hmm.*" Cheryl sat back in her chair and tried to think. It sounded like Jeff really did want to make sure things happened fairly but that his hands were tied. He seemed like a decent guy. Too bad that didn't get her any closer to the bottom of this. If only there was a way to figure out how the buyer had known the title was missing, or to know how it had disappeared from the county's records.

"Is it possible to see the records?" Cheryl asked. "Or I guess, where the records should be?"

"Sure. I can introduce you to Carolyn Caldwell, the clerk, who oversees the actual records rooms. Her team is also in charge of the digital archive, so she might be able to answer any questions you might have about that."

"That would be wonderful. Thank you."

He grabbed another handful of jelly beans and tossed them into his mouth, and then he pushed himself up and walked around his desk. She followed him out the doorway and into the hall, and they chatted about his wife, Jessica, and how interesting she found her job driving the Amish. They walked down a set of stairs to the second floor and then a long hallway until they stopped in front of a doorway marked Vital Records. Jeff pushed it open as they entered, and a woman looked up from a computer at a tall counter. Behind her was a door and a bank of windows, and beyond that, Cheryl saw, was a large room filled with floor-to-ceiling metal filing cabinets.

"Hi, Carolyn. This is Cheryl Cooper. She's Mitzi Porter's niece and runs the Swiss Miss over in Sugarcreek. She has a question about the land we got that strange offer on yesterday."

"Sure thing." Carolyn was probably in her midforties, small and petite with brown hair cut in a fashionable bob lightened with blonde highlights. "I can take care of her from here, Jeff," she said, and Jeff nodded, told Cheryl to call him anytime if she had any more questions, and headed back out.

"So you're interested in that parcel of land over by the creek," she said. Her voice was not unkind, but she was a bit guarded.

"Yes, my friend Levi Miller was saving up to buy the land from his uncle Silas, and then it turns out when Silas passed, he left the land to Levi in his will. But they were told yesterday that there's no record of Silas owning that land, so I'm trying to get to the bottom of it."

Carolyn nodded. "I was very surprised when we discovered that yesterday. We record every land transaction in the county, so when Jeff asked me to pull the records for this plot of land, I was shocked to see there was no record of it. You don't see that much anymore, not with land going for the prices they do these days."

"So there's just no record of it at all?" Cheryl still couldn't understand this bit. "Isn't that strange?"

Carolyn shrugged. "It's rare, but this is a large county. Not every single acre of farmland can be accounted for."

This answer didn't satisfy Cheryl. If no one else owned the land, it should have been owned by the county, she thought. Wouldn't the county have a record of all its holdings?

"Is there any chance the record might have been misplaced or misfiled?"

"Not likely," Carolyn said with a note of defensiveness in her voice. "We keep very careful records here."

Cheryl cringed, realizing Carolyn had taken offense. Of course, she could see how it sounded as if Cheryl had been questioning whether she did her job correctly.

"I'm sorry, I didn't mean any offense," Cheryl said. "I'm sure you do a fantastic job. I'm just trying to understand how it all works."

Carolyn nodded, placated at least for now.

"Would it be possible to see the records?"

Carolyn gave her another wary glance, and Cheryl continued, "Just so I understand a bit more. I'd like to be able to explain the system to my Amish friends so they know what's happening."

Carolyn let out a breath, showing her frustration, but then she turned her computer screen so Cheryl could see it and logged on to the records database. Her manicured fingers flew over the keys.

"See?" she said, typing the name *Silas Miller* into one of the fields on the screen. The search turned up parcels of land owned by dozens of Millers, but the only plot owned by Silas Miller, according to these records, was the one next to Levi's plot, the one with the house on it. She then tried the search several different ways—using the name of the road the land bordered, the name of the creek, and even the lot number she got from a mapping program on her computer.

"Would you like to see where the paper records should be too?" Carolyn asked.

"If that's not too much trouble, that would be helpful," Cheryl said, giving her best endearing smile.

Carolyn sighed, but then she hopped down off her high stool and gestured for Cheryl to follow. Cheryl walked around the counter and went behind Carolyn through the heavy door. Inside the records room, the air was dry and still, and it was so quiet their footsteps echoed on the wooden floor. Rows of filing cabinets ran along each wall and in two rows down the middle of the room.

"You've got a lot of files in here," Cheryl said to break the silence.

Carolyn turned back and gave her a forced smile.

"We keep track of a lot of things here. Not just deeds and title transfers but lots of other things." She turned back around then continued down the row, her tailored skirt swishing with each step.

Cheryl nodded. Apparently Carolyn was not going to tell her what those things were. No matter. She stopped in front of a bank of drawers about halfway down the row and pointed at a drawer.

"The certificate of title should be in here," she said, pulling open a drawer. Cheryl saw that it was stuffed full of hanging file folders. Carolyn flipped through the marked tabs on the top of the folders and indicated a spot between two folders. "If we had anything, it would go here."

"And you checked in the folders around it, to make sure it wasn't misplaced?"

Carolyn shot her a withering glare. "Yes, I did." She pushed the drawer closed with a thud.

"Who all has access to these files?" Cheryl asked.

Carolyn started walking back toward the door to the front room, and Cheryl followed a few steps behind.

"This room is open to the public, so it's hard to say," Carolyn said. Her heels clicked against the floor as she made her way back.

"So there's not any way to know who might have looked at the file, or when?"

"I think it's more likely that there wasn't a file in the first place," she said, pulling open the door. "Since there's no electronic record..." Her voice trailed off, making it clear exactly what she thought.

"Have you ever had a file simply vanish like this before?" Cheryl asked. She stepped through the door and out into the front part of the office.

"I've been doing this job for fifteen years," Carolyn said, pulling the door shut behind her. "And no, in that time, I have never misplaced a file or a record."

Well then. That made her opinion clear, Cheryl supposed. "Well, thank you for looking," Cheryl said, injecting her voice with false cheerfulness. While her natural inclination was to answer prickliness with attitude of her own, she knew it wasn't exactly Christlike... And not only that, you could catch more flies with honey than with vinegar, as her Southern momma liked to say.

"Anytime," Carolyn said, climbing back up onto her stool.

Based on how Carolyn's mood had soured over the course of their conversation, she very much doubted that Carolyn meant it, but Cheryl smiled and thanked her again anyway, and then she headed out the door.

The whole drive back to Sugarcreek, Cheryl couldn't stop thinking about how the title could have gone missing. Or was it possible that Silas Miller hadn't owned the land after all? Like Jeff had said, it was unlikely that an Amish man would make something like that up—and it was even more unlikely that he would have been able to get away with using the land all this time if it was not his. But was it possible he was mistaken? Could he have thought he owned it, but had the details wrong, or—she hated to even think it—could he have been swindled when he thought he bought it?

Cheryl parked in the small lot in front of the Swiss Miss and unlocked the front door. She was just in time to open the shop for the day, and soon after she turned on the lights and got the register ready, a busload of tourists came in. She was thankful when Lydia Troyer came in for her shift. Lydia was a good friend of Esther Miller's, and she too had been picking up extra hours as the busy summer tourist season took hold.

"This is such a cute store," an older woman said as Cheryl rang up a set of pot holders made by Joanna Hochstetler, one of Cheryl's Amish suppliers. Cheryl had already gathered from chatting with some other women that this group had come from a church in Cincinnati, and Cheryl thanked her. Then she explained that her aunt Mitzi owned the store, but Cheryl had taken it over when Mitzi heeded the Lord's call and went to Papua New Guinea as a missionary.

"Well then I love it even more," the woman said, smiling as she handed over her credit card. Cheryl rang up a few more items, including handmade soap and small toys whittled by more Amish friends, and then the store quieted down. Ben and Rueben Vogel had come in during the rush and were playing checkers at the small table by the front window, so Cheryl waved but didn't want to interrupt their game by talking to them.

"How are you doing, Lydia?" Cheryl asked after she'd had a moment to catch her breath.

"Groovy," Lydia said. Cheryl laughed. Lydia had decided to join the church but was technically still in her running-around years, and she loved trying out different English phrases and sayings. This one, however, seemed to be from an era Cheryl suspected she wouldn't be as fond of.

"Glad to hear it."

Lydia picked up a dust cloth and started tidying the store. Despite her little rebellions, Lydia was still Amish at heart, as evidenced by the fact that she hadn't needed to be asked how to fill her time between rushes. Like most Amish, Lydia was a very hard worker.

Cheryl decided to take advantage of the few quiet moments to return some e-mails, and she stepped toward the counter at the back of the store and logged on to her laptop computer. She responded to a few questions and placed orders for a few non-Amish-made items she needed to restock. Then her mind drifted back to Silas Miller and his land.

Was it possible Silas truly hadn't owned that land? Or was someone trying to steal it from him? She wondered how she could find out.

Well, she could start with the obvious, she supposed. She opened up a browser window and typed the name *Silas Miller* into a search engine. As she'd expected, most of the results that came up had little to do with the recently deceased Amish man. Silas hadn't had much of an online presence, which made sense, considering the Amish didn't use computers for the most part. Still, on the second page of results, there was one link that looked interesting. Cheryl clicked on it and saw that it was a Yelp page for something called Miller Furniture in Sugarcreek. The address listed matched the number of the house Cheryl had seen earlier when Carolyn showed her the files.

Cheryl had used the Web site Yelp before. It was a place where consumers could leave reviews for various businesses. Cheryl had often used the site to check out what customers said about restaurants she'd wanted to try when she lived in Columbus and to find things like hair salons and dry cleaners that did a good job.

Cheryl looked at the entry for Miller Furniture and saw that Silas seemed to have upholstered and refinished furniture out of a workshop attached to his house. The customer reviews were stellar, almost entirely five stars, and several people had commented on how professional his work was, while others praised his low prices and honesty. Several people mentioned that he was a quirky person, but kind. One person said he'd done a fine job refinishing a family heirloom rocking chair, and another had loved his work on re-covering a couch.

Huh. Cheryl wished she'd found this page before Silas passed away. She had an armchair that needed to be reupholstered, and it seemed he'd been the perfect person to do the job. Too bad.

Cheryl thought it was funny that this Amish man's business had Yelp reviews, but aside from that, she hadn't learned much from her Internet research. She wasn't sure what else she was looking for, so she sat back and thought about what the next step was.

Well, if someone really was trying to steal the land from Levi, there was one obvious person she should call. She didn't even have to look up the number before she placed the call. A few minutes later, she was connected to Chief Twitchell, the police chief in Sugarcreek.

"Hi, Chief. I'm wondering if you can help me," Cheryl said. Her mind worked quickly, trying to figure out the best way to ask this.

"I can try." His voice held just a hint of a soft Southern accent.

"I think someone might be trying to steal land from Levi Miller."

There was a pause and then a sigh. "You *think* someone *might* be *trying* to?"

When he said it like that, Cheryl realized how flimsy it sounded. "Yes. And I'm wondering what can be done about it."

"Well, I don't really know what I can do if you're not even sure a theft has taken place."

"Can you help me stop it?"

"Uh...how exactly would I do that?" The police chief's voice sounded weary.

"I..." Cheryl thought about this. "Well, I don't know exactly. Someone took the evidence that his uncle Silas owned a piece of land out of the county files. I'm trying to figure out who before the county sells the land out from under him."

He was quiet for a minute. Cheryl heard typing on his end of the line.

"You know I want to make sure no one gets away with theft around here, but it sounds like this case isn't quite ready for the police yet," he said. "It sounds more like what you need is a lawyer. If there is doubt about the ownership of the land, a good lawyer should be able to block any sale until the ownership question is cleared up."

She wanted to argue with him, but she realized he was right. A lawyer probably was the logical next step, though she had a feeling she knew exactly what her Amish friends would think of that.

"Thank you for your help," Cheryl said.

"Of course. Let me know if there's anything else I can do."

She hung up the phone and looked up.

"Oh, hello, Esther."

She'd been so wrapped up in her search she hadn't even noticed that Esther had arrived for her shift.

"Hello, Cheryl. How are you?" The girl was adjusting her *kapp*, and she was a bit out of breath.

"I'm okay. How's everyone at your house?"

Cheryl was especially wondering how Levi was faring, but she didn't want to come out and ask about him directly.

"They are fine, but I chose to ride my bike in today so that Levi would not forget me again." She made a face and laughed. "They are all busy anyway. We will host the funeral for Uncle Silas at our house this Thursday, and my father and brothers spent the morning digging the grave, and *Maam* is very busy getting things ready to host the service."

"Wait, I'm sorry...What?" Cheryl couldn't have heard that right. "Digging the grave?"

"Yes, digging the grave. Over at the Amish cemetery." Esther slipped a red Swiss Miss apron on over her head and tied the strings at her waist.

"Like, with shovels?" Cheryl was incredulous.

"Of course." Esther shrugged. "How else would it get dug?"

Cheryl hadn't really thought about that. It wasn't like they could use a backhoe. But the idea of digging a grave—and by hand—was difficult to imagine.

"Oh, and Levi and Daed were hoping you could stop by our house after lunch. They want to go to Uncle Silas's house to look for the missing deed, and they were hoping you might be able to help."

"Of course, I'm happy to. Thanks for letting me know."

The shop was still mostly empty, and Cheryl realized her stomach was rumbling. Now would be a good time to run out to get something to eat, and then she would head over to the Miller farm.

"I'm going to run out for a bit," she said, and both Amish girls nodded and then started chatting in Pennsylvania Dutch. Esther was already running a dust cloth over a display of handcrafted games and puzzles. Both were hard workers, and she knew they could handle whatever crowds showed up while she was gone.

Cheryl waved before stepping out of the shop and into the bright June sunshine. The sun was high, and the day was hot. But without a trace of humidity, the air felt soft and light. Cheryl waved at Ezra Wittmer, who owned the Old Amish Store, as he unhitched his buggy, and then she carefully crossed the busy Route 39 and walked up the steps to the Honey Bee. The rich scent of coffee greeted her as she crossed the porch and entered the café. This place was hopping. Every table was taken, mostly by what looked like tourists. She recognized a few of the women who had come into her shop earlier, and she waved and got in line at the counter. The space was open and bright, with small vases of flowers on each of the tables spread across the dining area. The menu was printed on chalkboards hung on the back wall; the display cases were filled with locally sourced croissants, donuts, and muffins, as well as bagels and freshly baked bread; and the whole placed smelled like earthy coffee.

When it was finally her turn, Cheryl stepped up to the counter and ordered a ham-and-cheese sandwich and cup of iced tea.

"You sure you don't want to make that a latte? It's your last chance for a few days," said Kathy Snyder, the owner of the Honey Bee. Kathy's smile was warm, and Cheryl thought how much she had come to treasure Kathy's friendship since she'd moved to Sugarcreek.

"What do you mean?"

"I have to head out of town," Kathy said, pulling one of the premade ham-and-cheese sandwiches out of the display case. Cheryl knew Kathy had made it only a few hours ago, and it was bursting with fresh-cured ham from local farmers and sharp swiss cheese from Heini's Cheese Chalet, a local Amish favorite. "My mother had a fall, and I'm going to Cleveland to take care of her for a few days. I'll be gone until at least Saturday. And Heather has the week off, and Bella quit last week." Now that she mentioned it, Cheryl didn't see either of the girls who were usually helping ferry dishes from tables to the back of the café.

"I'm so sorry to hear that," Cheryl said. "And not just because I will miss your coffee. I'll take that latte after all." She smiled and continued, "Is your mother okay?"

"She's going to be, but she's uncomfortable, and she'll need some help getting around for the next few days. I'm hoping to help however I can." She set the sandwich on a plate and slid it across the counter.

"Well, I'm sure it will be a comfort to her to have you there."

"I hope so." Kathy moved over to the espresso machine and pulled the lever to let espresso powder fall into the filter. "Unfortunately, it means I'm going to have to close up shop." She pushed a button, and a moment later warm espresso streamed out of the machine into the waiting cup.

"That is unfortunate." Cheryl looked around at the packed tables and the line that had formed behind her. "Especially this time of year." Cheryl knew that most of the businesses in the Sugarcreek area did fine year-round, but they relied on a sizeable chunk of their income during the summer months.

"It is too bad, but it can't be helped, I'm afraid. I wish there was some other solution, but I just can't afford to hire anyone to take over while I'm out—let alone train them in time." She poured steamed milk from a metal jug into the paper cup and slipped a lid on top.

"Well, you will be missed," Cheryl said. She reached for the coffee, and as Kathy rang up her lunch, an idea started to form in Cheryl's mind. Could she . . . But no, that would be too much, too huge a task.

But . . . She looked around the little café. It would be such a blessing to Kathy, not to mention to the people of Sugarcreek and the visitors who came through.

Kathy announced her total, and Cheryl handed over her cash. She eyed the display cases and the jugs of coffee. How hard could it be, really?

Kathy handed back her change, and as Cheryl settled down at a recently vacated table by the door, she mulled over the idea. It would take some work to pull it all together, but once the pieces were in place, it shouldn't be all that difficult. It would only be for a few days. Cheryl was sure she could do it.

By the time Cheryl had finished her sandwich and was placing the empty plate in the bin over the trash can, she had come up with a plan.

Chapter Three

A few minutes later, Cheryl pulled up into the driveway for the Miller farm. On this bright summer day, the petting zoo the family operated was busy, and Cheryl navigated around several minivans and a mother with small children as she pulled up close to the house. Just past the parking area was a large horse-drawn wagon, which would take visitors to view the pens of pygmy goats and miniature horses beyond the barns. Cheryl waved at Eli Miller, who was waiting to drive the wagon, and she looked around. Eighteen-year-old Elizabeth Miller crouched down at the entrance to the pen that held chickens and ducks, talking to a group of preschoolers. Rover sat nearby, enjoying the attention a group of children was giving him. Out in the field, she saw what she thought was Seth, guiding a horse-drawn plow through the rows. Cheryl didn't see Levi or Naomi anywhere, so she headed toward the house and knocked on the door.

"Come in, please," Cheryl heard from inside. Cheryl pushed open the door and stepped inside. Despite the heat outside, Naomi's house was cool, even without air-conditioning, and it smelled like heaven. "In the kitchen," Naomi called.

"Goodness." When Cheryl stepped into the kitchen, she found Naomi elbow-deep in a giant bowl of some sort of dough. There were at least half a dozen fruit pies cooling on the table, and a small mountain of green beans sat on the counter, waiting to be trimmed.

"Are you cooking for an army?"

When Naomi's family all gathered together, it was enough to make up a baseball team, and Cheryl was used to seeing her cook for large groups, but this was a bit much, even for Naomi.

"I am sorry I could not come to the door," Naomi said, nodding at the bowl of dough. "Thank you for seeing yourself in." She gestured for Cheryl to take a seat at the table.

"Of course." Cheryl lowered herself into a chair. There was a blueberry peach pie just in front of her, and the sweet juice had bubbled up through the flaky crust. "What's going on?"

"We are having the funeral for Silas here on Thursday and the visitation on Wednesday," Naomi said. "So I am making biscuits."

"Ah." That explained it. Cheryl had never been to an Amish funeral, but she had been to enough Amish gatherings to know that a meal was always involved. "You're hosting the services here, in the house?"

"Yes, in the living room," Naomi said. A year ago, this would have surprised Cheryl, but by now she was used to the way the Amish took turns holding their worship services in members' houses instead of at a church building. In that light, it sort of made sense that a funeral would be held in a house instead of in a funeral home or church. And if preparing to host a funeral was anything like prepping to host church, Cheryl knew the house would be cleaned top to bottom as well as a feast prepared.

"Is there anything I can do to help?" The blueberry peach pie in front of her smelled so good. She took a deep inhale, and then she tried to ignore it.

"Not with the funeral arrangements, but thank you," Naomi said. She dug her hands deep into the biscuit batter, using her fingers to mix it together. "Some of the women in the church are helping with the food, and the men are helping Seth and Levi with the chores and with digging the grave as we prepare, so we have plenty of help in that way." She pulled a handful of dough from the bowl and examined it, judging its consistency.

"But Levi is grateful you are willing to help get the land. Seth and Levi were going to go over to Silas's house soon and were hoping you could go too."

"Of course," Cheryl said. "I'm not sure how much help I can be searching Silas's house, but I am willing to try."

"It is always good to have another set of eyes," Naomi said, turning the ball of dough over in the bowl. "And you sometimes think of things that we would never think of."

Cheryl had to laugh at that. "Yes, I suppose I do see things differently sometimes."

"And that is why we like you."

Cheryl hesitated. "If you really want my help, I can tell you what I think would be the best thing for you to do, but I suspect you won't like it."

"What is that?"

Again, she hesitated. The Amish were famously nonlitigious and avoided legal intervention in their disputes whenever possible.

"Have you thought about hiring a lawyer to try to block the sale? That would probably be the first thing I would recommend."

"I do not know." She dropped the ball of dough back into the bowl and used her hands to mix it. "I do not think Seth will want to do that."

"I suspected that. But it might be the best thing."

Naomi didn't say anything for a moment. Then, simply, "I will talk to him about it."

Naomi turned the dough again, set it down, and nodded. "There. That is ready. I will go get Levi." Naomi wiped her hands on her apron and then moved over to the back door and pulled it open. Cheryl turned and saw that Levi was out in the backyard, fixing something on the gate that led to the small vegetable garden.

"Cheryl is here. Please call your daed," Cheryl heard Naomi say through the open door. Levi said something back to her in Pennsylvania Dutch, and then he started off toward the field.

Naomi came back inside and studied the pies on the table.

"I think I need at least three more."

"How many people are you expecting?" Cheryl laughed. It was too tempting. She pushed the pie aside and tried to focus on her friend.

"It is hard to say. Some of Seth's family is coming down from Michigan. So at least ten of them, plus us. Plus many people from our community here. Silas was well liked." Naomi shrugged. "Maybe fifty or sixty? Perhaps more."

Cheryl tried to imagine fifty or sixty people inside this house. It was a large house, but still it would be tight.

"Do you have to cook all this though? I've been at funerals where there were just light refreshments afterward, and it was fine." Cheryl's father was a pastor out in Seattle, Washington, and she had been to her fair share of funerals over the years. "Surely you don't have to feed all of them."

"Of course I don't have to feed all of them," Naomi said. "Others will bring food too. But I want to make sure we have enough. People will be traveling from far away and taking time off work. It would not do to run out of food."

Cheryl shook her head. "I don't know how you do it."

"We just do it. It is our way."

Cheryl didn't always understand the ways of her Amish friends, but she did appreciate the way the community always seemed to come together to support each other, no matter the circumstances.

Just then the back door opened again, and Levi stepped inside, followed by his father Seth. Both men had used the outdoor pump to wash their faces and hands, and their cheeks were pink and fresh looking. Levi wiped his hands on his pants as they came inside.

"Thank you for coming with us," Levi said. Seth nodded, adding his thanks to his son's.

"I'm happy to do it." Cheryl stood and hitched her purse over her shoulder. "Shall we take my car?"

Both men looked at each other, and Seth nodded. "If you do not mind, that will be faster."

"Of course I don't mind." She turned to Naomi. "Are you coming too?"

"No, I must stay here and continue to prepare. But you will be very helpful. Thank you for going."

"Happy to." She turned to the men. "Ready?"

They followed her out to her car. Levi let his father take the front, and she laughed as both tall men struggled to fit themselves into her compact car. When they were all buckled up, she turned the car around, waving at Elizabeth, and pulled out.

"You all went over to the house last evening," Cheryl said. "But I guess you didn't find anything?" She wanted to know where things stood, but she also asked partly to fill the quiet. As comfortable as Cheryl felt with Levi, he was still a man of few words, and Seth did not typically speak much at all, at least in her presence.

"I went mostly to milk my brother's cows, but while I was there, I found the will, which was in my brother's files, exactly where it was supposed to be," Seth said. "And the title for the house and the land around it was there. But the property title for the other plot of land was not there. My brother was..." He paused, thinking. His silence stretched on for a beat too long, but Cheryl had learned not to interrupt. What felt like an awkwardly long time of quiet to her was simply the time Seth needed to choose the right words so he wouldn't regret what he said. "My brother was a good businessman, but not the most organized with keeping his records. You will see."

Oh dear. Now Cheryl wasn't sure what to expect.

"There is a safe in my uncle's office," Levi said. "But we do not know the combination. Maybe it is in there. We were hoping you might be able to help us figure it out."

Cheryl laughed. "I'm no locksmith."

"But you are good at puzzles."

Cheryl glanced at Levi in the rearview mirror and saw that he was watching her in the glass, admiration written clearly on his face. Cheryl's stomach warmed, and she looked away quickly. She couldn't let herself get distracted by...well, by the good-looking Amish man in her backseat.

Becoming Amish was not in her future. Becoming English was not in his. There was no way around it.

"I read online that Silas had a furniture business," Cheryl said to break the silence again.

"Yes, he was very skilled. He could upholster anything," Levi said.

"You learned this online?" Seth asked, chuckling. "My brother would find that funny."

The car got quiet again, except for the few times Seth indicated where she should turn, so Cheryl stopped fighting it and contemplated what her friends back in Columbus would think if they saw her now, driving two Amish men in hats and suspenders through cornfields.

"What is that noise?" Levi asked.

"What noise?" Cheryl asked.

"That squealing. It is coming from your car."

Cheryl listened, and then she heard it, a high-pitched whine coming from under the hood. "Oh, that? It's been doing that for a while. It's nothing to worry about."

"You have taken it to a mechanic?" Levi asked.

"Not yet, but I will soon. But like I said, it's been making that noise for a while and nothing bad happens, so I'm sure it's fine."

Cheryl saw the men exchange glances.

"I think you should make sure to get it checked out," Levi said. "Just to be safe."

"All right," Cheryl promised. "I will."

And she would, at some point, but…well, two Amish men weren't exactly high on her list of people to take car advice from. If she ever needed advice about a horse-drawn buggy, they were the first people she'd turn to, but she felt sure she knew a thing or two more than they did about cars.

"It is just up there," Seth said, pointing to a small one-story white house and a barn set back from the road. A hand-lettered sign that said Miller Furniture was parked at the end of the driveway. Cheryl slowed down and turned into the dirt driveway, taking in the mature oaks that shaded the house and the lovely small creek that ran a few hundred feet to the side by the garden.

"This is charming," Cheryl said as they stepped out of the car. Cheryl saw that a small workshop was attached to the house, and the door for the furniture business was separate from the main door to the house. She had seen this at several Amish homes that had businesses attached.

"He lived here all alone?" Cheryl asked.

"Since his wife died, about three years ago," Seth said. "They never had children, and we offered for him to move in with us but he preferred to be here."

Cheryl nodded. This place was peaceful. She could see why Silas had chosen to stay here.

"Uncle Emmon will inherit the house and all the land out to that row of trees," Levi said, pointing to a grove of poplars a few hundred yards away. "The land I was saving to buy goes from those trees to the next road, and back as far as that hill," he said, gesturing behind the house. It was a large piece of property, more than enough for Levi to build his own house and farm, and it really was a beautiful spot.

"The land you will inherit, you mean," Cheryl said. "We *will* find proof that your uncle owned it."

Seth led them to the front door of the house and stepped inside. As both Seth and Levi took off their hats, Cheryl took in the wide-plank floors, the simple wooden furniture, and the handmade cabinetry in the kitchen. On the walls were some paintings of flowers and a few embroidered sayings. A colorful quilt was draped over the back of a rocking chair in the open living space. These decorative touches were remnants of Silas's wife, Cheryl felt certain. Everything in this house appeared to be humble but well-crafted.

"Most of his records were kept in the office area at the back," Seth said. He hung his hat on a hook by the door and started down the hallway that branched off to the right. Cheryl followed him through the living room, past a small closet and two bedrooms, and into a large room with a desk and chair. Half a dozen metal filing cabinets were pushed against the walls, and a closed door was set into the far wall. The Amish equivalent of a home office.

"This is where he kept his business records." Seth gestured around the room. There was a window that looked out over the front yard, and the walls were creamy white and bare, except for one small piece of muslin with the scripture, "Beloved, let us love one another" cross-stitched in dark blue thread. "And the workshop is through here." He pushed open the door and stepped into the workshop, and Cheryl moved to the doorway and looked out. It was a large, garagelike space, with high, unfinished ceilings and rows of metal shelving against the walls. Bolts of heavy upholstery fabric in bright, cheerful colors were stacked up against one wall, attesting to the fact that his clients were not all Amish. In the center of the room was a workspace with a high table and various tools scattered about. A few pieces of furniture in various stages of repair were left in the room, and the smells of sawdust and wood stain hung in the air.

"Where did you find his will?" Cheryl asked, stepping back into the office.

"That was with his personal papers, which he kept in his desk drawer," Seth said, and he indicated the large lower drawer on the desk. Levi pulled it open, and Cheryl saw that it was stuffed full of file folders, each crammed with papers. Cheryl leaned down and ran her fingers along the tabs on the folders, finally stopping at one marked: Important Papers.

"Well, that's fairly direct, isn't it?" Cheryl laughed, but the Amish men did not. There was no accounting for taste.

She pulled out the folder and laid it on the desk and then opened it. Inside, Cheryl found a copy of what was clearly the will, as well as a government photo ID, the transaction papers for his horses, and a deed and accompanying paperwork for the house and main plot of land. There were also copies of his past seven years' tax returns and some health records. It was all very neat and orderly, and also, Cheryl had to admit, thorough. It was exactly the kind of paperwork you would expect someone to have in a folder like this, and because the other papers in the folder were so complete, the omission of the deed for the land was even more glaring.

"Okay. So where else did he keep important things?" Cheryl said, her voice just a shade more upbeat than she felt. "I suppose we'll have to look through the filing cabinets?"

Seth nodded. "My brother kept a record for every piece of furniture he worked on in the time he ran his business. That is over forty years of records," he said, indicating the filing cabinets. "But I cannot figure out his filing system, so if you can, I will be very pleased."

"Oh boy." Cheryl pulled open one of the drawers on the top cabinet and saw that the first four folders it contained were labeled Abramowitz, Huffman, Perry, and Long. There did not seem to be any obvious organizing system, but Cheryl knew there had to be one. The meticulous way the folder marked Important Papers was kept made her certain these were arranged in some way that made sense, if only to Silas. But it was going to be a challenge sorting through all these folders without knowing what his logic had been. There had to be at least a hundred folders just in this drawer alone, and there were twenty-three more drawers.

"There is the safe," Seth said, indicating a small dark gray safe Cheryl hadn't noticed before, mostly hidden behind the desk. "I do not know the combination though."

Cheryl crouched and examined it. It had a dial lock with numbers marked out by little white lines all the way to one hundred. The dial spun smoothly.

Cheryl stood up and looked around the room. "Okay. We have to get this thing open. The deed could be inside. The combination for this safe has got to be here somewhere. Maybe I'll poke around in the desk and see if I can find anything?"

Seth nodded. "I will start looking through the workshop. Levi, you can search other parts of the house."

"Is there much chance he left it in another part of the house?" Cheryl asked. She supposed anything was possible, but why would he leave it in the cookie jar or something when all of his other papers were so well organized?

No one answered for a moment, and then, after a beat too long, Levi said, "It would not have been Uncle Silas who hid it."

"What do you mean?"

Seth took a deep breath and then let it out. "My brother's wife had started showing signs of dementia before she passed away."

"She more than started. She had it, for certain," Levi clarified.

"Oh dear. I'm sorry." Cheryl had watched her own grandfather suffer from Alzheimer's, and she knew it was a terrible disease and very difficult for the family.

"She had many struggles, especially toward the end," Seth said. "And she often moved things around so my brother did not know where they were."

"What do you mean?"

"He means that sometimes Uncle Silas would find the iron in the icebox, or she'd hang her laundry to dry inside the outhouse. That sort of thing."

Ah. Now Cheryl could see what he was getting at. "So there's a chance the title is hidden somewhere totally random."

"There is a chance," Levi acknowledged.

"How long ago did she get moved to assisted living?"

Both men stared at her. Levi tilted his head.

"She lived here until she passed away three years ago," Levi said. "We do not send people to assisted living," he continued. "We believe families should take care of the people who took care of them."

Ah. Now that he mentioned it, that seemed much more like how the Amish would do it, and it also seemed very appealing. How would Grandpa Bill's later years have been different if he'd lived at home, cared for not by nurses but by his family? Cheryl knew it had been impossible for her father to care for his father as well as the dedicated nurses had, but the Amish made it work... Well, she'd have to think about that more later. For now, she needed to focus on the task at hand.

"Did she have any favorite hiding places?" If she had passed away three years ago, it seemed unlikely that there were still things hidden here and there, especially considering how orderly the rest of the house was, but you never could tell.

Seth nodded. "There is a loose brick in the fireplace. We found a bunch of coupons there yesterday when we looked."

"And there was a bag of fabric scraps in one of the kitchen drawers," Levi added.

"Okay." Cheryl tried to think. "So it could be anywhere."

"It could," Levi said. "It does not seem the most likely thing, but it is possible."

"Levi, I think you should go search for hiding spots throughout the house while Cheryl works in here," Seth said.

"I will do that in a while. First I will try to figure out if there is anything in these filing cabinets, since that seems more likely," Levi said, already bending over the drawer Cheryl had pulled open.

Seth hesitated. Cheryl knew he was not used to being second-guessed by his children, even grown men like Levi, and he seemed like he might be about to say something. He looked from Levi to Cheryl. But then he let out a breath, nodded, and simply turned and walked into the workshop.

Cheryl worried a bit about his reaction, but Levi did not seem concerned, so Cheryl just sat down in the desk chair and started opening drawers. Cheryl always kept her important passwords on sticky notes inside her desk. She knew it wasn't the most secure thing to do, but passwords had to be changed so often these days, and she couldn't keep track of them, so she wrote them down. She was hoping Silas had done something similar. In the small drawer in the center of the desk, she found pens and pencils and several small notepads, as well as a solar-powered calculator, but none of the notepads had anything that looked like a combination on them. There was also a handful of business cards—one for a lumber company, a farrier, and one, oddly, for a Michael Borland from Borland Developers with an office in Canton.

Cheryl knew what this was. There was no proof, of course, but Cheryl felt sure this had to be the developer who was now trying to buy the land. So this Michael Borland had been in contact with Silas, it seemed. But why?

The card was a bit faded and the edges were worn, as if it had been in there a while. Still, it was odd enough that she decided to pull out her phone and take a quick picture of it. Then she turned to the top drawer on the right and found stamps, envelopes, and return address labels. Nothing useful there.

"I think I figured out his filing system," Levi said. Cheryl looked up. She hadn't forgotten Levi was in the room. She was too aware of his presence to have forgotten, but she had gotten so absorbed in her search that she was surprised to hear him speak.

"Really?" Cheryl brightened.

"I think each filing cabinet is a type of furniture," Levi said. "This one seems to hold folders for chairs he repaired. This one"— he indicated the cabinet next to it—"is for couches he'd upholstered. And I think this one is for ottomans and footstools." He touched a third cabinet. "And inside each cabinet, they're organized by date, with the most recent projects on top."

"What an odd way to keep your files," Cheryl said, shaking her head.

"It's not the way most people do it, but if you think about it, it actually makes sense," Levi said. "Uncle Silas was ... well, I guess the *Englisch* would say quirky. We might say he was a bit *ab im kopp*, though he was plenty smart. He just thought about things differently. He liked numbers and could remember dates but had a hard time with faces. If he was trying to keep track of his projects, he would be sure to think about the piece of furniture itself first and then the rough date he had worked on the project. The name of the customer would be the last thing he would remember."

It sounded to Cheryl like Silas might have had a touch of Asperger's syndrome, a form of high-functioning autism. If that was the case, his filing system might actually make a kind of sense.

"It may have made it easier for him to find things, but it sure doesn't help us," Cheryl said.

"This is true," Levi said. "Though truth be told, I do not exactly know what I am looking for. Just anything that looks odd or like it might lead to the deed."

Cheryl nodded. She wasn't exactly sure what he might find in the files either, and if they had to sort through each individual file, it would take them months, but she agreed they had to at least try. "I will keep looking," Levi said, and Cheryl smiled and nodded then turned back to the desk.

She pulled open the big bottom drawer, hung with filing folders, and she started sorting through. In addition to the folder marked Important Papers, there were folders containing paperwork for various aspects of his business and for various types of bills. Cheryl sorted through it all but didn't find anything that looked like a deed or a combination for the safe.

Okay, so if the combination wasn't recorded in the desk, it could be somewhere else in the house, or it might not have been written down anywhere. If that was the case, it must have been some number that was memorable to him.

"What was your uncle's birthday?" Cheryl asked.

"November 28, 1947," Levi said.

Huh. She spun the dial to the 11, and then back the other way to 28, and then to 47. That didn't work. She tried again with 1-1-28, but she didn't hear anything. She pulled on the handle just to be sure, but it didn't budge.

"What about his wife's birthday?" Cheryl asked, knowing it was probably futile. She knew Aunt Mitzi's birth date, but she wouldn't have been able to list the birthday of any of her other aunts or uncles.

"May 29, 1956," Levi said.

"It seems like Silas wasn't the only one good at numbers," Cheryl said, smiling.

Levi shrugged. "People are important to us."

By "us" she knew he meant the Amish, and from her time in Sugarcreek, she knew it to be true. Cheryl tried 5-29-56 and then 5-2-9, but nothing happened.

"Can you think of any other significant dates? Or numbers that were important to your uncle?"

Levi paused and looked up from the folder he was sorting through.

"His father was born March 10, 1924. Maybe try that?"

Cheryl tried 3-10-24 and then, at Levi's suggestion, Silas and Betty's wedding date, but nothing worked. Cheryl turned the dial in her hand, her eyes roaming around the room. She took in the plain white walls, the window hung with dark curtains, the Bible verse cross-stitched on the wall...nothing useful. It would take days, maybe even weeks to try all the possible combinations. There had to be a better way.

"I think maybe we should call a locksmith."

"A locksmith?" Once again, Levi paused in his work. "To open the safe? How would that work?"

"I'm not sure, but I think they might have some method or tool to figure out the numbers. They listen to the dial turn or something." Cheryl wasn't exactly sure how it worked, but she knew she'd seen it happen on one of those cop shows on television. Not that Levi would have any experience with those. "Or they might be able to just take the door off."

"I am not sure we'd want to do that yet," Levi said.

"Why not? Don't you want to get into the safe?"

"Of course. But the safe belongs to Uncle Emmon now," Levi said patiently. "We cannot destroy it without his permission."

Cheryl felt frustration rise. Sometimes she really did not understand her Amish friends. If they didn't get this safe open, they might not find the deed they needed to prove Silas had owned the land. Surely Emmon would understand if they needed to bust open the safe?

"Well, how about I see if I can get a locksmith out here who won't have to take the door off?" Cheryl reached for her smartphone and did a quick search for locksmiths in the area, and she quickly came up with a name and phone number. While Levi kept combing through the files, she called the locksmith, an older guy with a thick Boston accent who said he was booked up this afternoon but he could come take a look at the safe the next day. Cheryl checked with Levi, who said that would work, and she agreed to meet him here the next afternoon at two.

Just then Seth came back in from the workshop. "It is getting late. We must go home and help with chores," he said.

"Did you find anything?" Levi asked, and Seth shook his head. "Me neither."

"We'll just have to keep looking. It's got to be here somewhere," Cheryl said, hoping she sounded more positive than she felt. Why hadn't Silas just kept the deed in a logical place, where a normal person would be able to find it? The county already had an offer on the land. Surely there would be a bit of time before they moved forward while the legal process went through all the proper channels, but Cheryl knew they would not hold off indefinitely. From the perspective of the county, there was no other claim on the land and thus no legal reason not to sell it. Cheryl knew they had to move quickly.

"I spoke with the police chief earlier, and he suggested getting a lawyer," Cheryl said. She'd tried with Naomi, but it wouldn't hurt to plant the idea in Seth's mind as well.

"I would prefer not to," he said simply.

"I understand that. But I think it might be the best way to make sure the county does not sell the land," Cheryl said.

"We do not need a lawyer. Not yet." Seth's answer was definite. Well, Cheryl would keep trying to find the deed for now and try again on the lawyer question later. They hadn't found Silas's copy of the deed yet, but Cheryl had a few other ideas for how to track it down.

As they drove back to the Miller farm, Cheryl asked Levi and Seth who else might have had access to Silas's house and office.

"His customers, perhaps," Levi said slowly.

"Ugh." Cheryl let out a groan. "I saw how many of them there are. It would take a year to talk to all of them. And they wouldn't have gone into the house or the office, would they? Wouldn't he have just met them in the workshop?"

"Yes, this is probably true," Seth admitted.

"Then let's not spin our wheels worrying about that just yet. Can you think of anyone else?"

She saw them look at each other in the rearview mirror.

"No one in our community would have taken it," Seth said simply.

"I believe that, but that wasn't my question," Cheryl said. She slowed as they crested a small hill and a buggy came into sight over the rise.

Neither of the men said anything for a moment. They looked at each other again. And then Cheryl understood what they weren't saying. Some Amish person had access, but they didn't want her to suspect that person.

"Of course I wouldn't suspect anyone of anything," Cheryl said. "But maybe they would have seen something that might be helpful. You could ask them, if you feel more comfortable with that." Cheryl slowed even further as she came up just behind the buggy, and she swung wide, steering around it. She gave a friendly wave to let the driver know she had seen him. She heard the horses' feet clip-clopping on the pavement.

Levi shifted in his seat and met his father's eyes in the rearview mirror again. That idea made him uncomfortable too, she could tell. Seth nodded at his son.

"Ruthanna Yutzy cleaned for him," Levi finally said.

Cheryl knew that it was fairly common for Amish girls to hire themselves out as housekeepers and cooks, especially to men who lived alone.

"Could I talk to her, just to see if she noticed anything that might be useful?" Cheryl asked. Safely past the horse and buggy, she sped up again.

"It would be better if you did than for us to," Seth said, though his face showed that he was still uncomfortable with the idea. "I will ask Naomi to put you in touch with her."

"That would be great," Cheryl said. She tapped her fingers on the steering wheel as she crested another hill. "Is there anyone else?"

The men were both silent for a moment. Cheryl tried to think. Who else might have a copy of the deed? And then it hit her, and it was so obvious she couldn't believe she'd missed it before.

"What about the lawyer who handled the sale of the land to Silas? He might have kept a copy of the paperwork. Do you know who that is?"

Seth didn't answer for a moment, and then, nodding, he said, "Yes. You could talk to the lawyer Luke Bradshaw."

She noticed that Levi flinched, almost involuntarily, at the name. "Luke Bradshaw?" she asked.

Seth nodded. "He drew up the will. It is likely he represented Silas when he bought the land as well. For many years he was one of the only lawyers in the area who worked with the Amish."

"That's perfect." Cheryl suddenly felt lighter. She didn't know if lawyers were required to keep copies of things like deeds when they handled a sale, but it was possible this Luke Bradshaw had exactly what they needed. "I'll talk to him."

She looked into the rearview mirror at Levi, who still had something of a sour look on his face. "Is there anything I should know about him?"

Once again, neither man said anything for a moment. She knew the Amish took the command in James not to spread gossip seriously, and they were prone to clam up when they didn't want to say anything bad about someone. She appreciated that but also found it difficult at times. How could they expect her to help them if they didn't tell her what she needed to know?

Levi sighed. "He does not have a good reputation among our people," he said simply.

"Why not?" Cheryl looked at him in the rearview mirror. "I thought you said he was one of the few lawyers who worked with the Amish. Why go to him if he had a bad reputation?"

"He has for many years been one of the few who would work with us," Seth explained carefully. "That is the main reason. But also, it is only in recent years that he has done some shady things.

Things that make us wary. But ten years ago, when my brother bought this land? It is likely he was involved."

"Shady things?" Cheryl asked.

Again, the pause. "Sometimes he charges more than he says he will, or he does not do what he promises," Levi said carefully.

Cheryl felt her blood pressure rise. She knew that sometimes people with a predatory streak saw the Amish as easy targets. And in some ways, maybe they were. Cheryl had met many Amish who were quite naïve about the ways of the outside world. But they were also, by and large, good, kind, generous people, and it made her angry to think about anyone taking advantage of them. She would talk to this Luke Bradshaw guy, and she would put him in his place while she was at it.

"Who did Silas buy the land from?" Cheryl asked. "That person might have some record of the sale."

Seth was nodding in the passenger seat. "That is a good idea. I do not remember his name, but I remember that he was an *Englischer* who tried his hand at farming for a while." He chuckled. "It did not take long for him to go back to the city, where he came from."

"It would be good to talk to him," Levi asked. "How can we find out his name?"

"Perhaps Henry King will remember. I believe it was his land before he sold it to the Englischer," Seth said. "He owns the house and land on the other side of Levi's land," he added by way of explanation.

Well, this should be easier than she'd thought. If they could find record of either Henry King or this Englisher owning the land, it should be simple enough to prove that the land had been owned by someone and therefore the empty records were false. The land didn't belong to the county. Simple enough.

By this time, they were nearing the Miller farm, and Cheryl slowed to make the turn into the driveway. Seth and Levi stepped out, and Seth promised to try to come up with the Englisher's name and to have Naomi put her in touch with Ruthanna Yutzy, and Cheryl said she would try to talk to the corrupt lawyer, Luke Bradshaw. Then she waved good-bye to the men, but instead of turning back toward Sugarcreek, Cheryl made a left out of the driveway and turned the other way. Before she headed back to the shop, there was someone else she wanted to talk to.

CHAPTER FOUR

It took a little more than thirty minutes to get to Canton, but Cheryl had programmed her phone's GPS with the address she'd gotten from the business card in Silas's desk, and she found the office easily. She pulled into the parking lot of a small business complex adjacent to a strip mall and parked near the front door. A quick scan of the directory showed Michael Borland's office was on the third floor of the building. A few minutes later, Cheryl was stepping through the glass door of the office. The floors were hardwood polished to a high sheen, and the walls were a bright white, hung with black-and-white photographs. A young woman with perfect blonde highlights looked up from the front desk and gave Cheryl a wary look.

"Hello. My name is Cheryl Cooper. I'd like to speak with Michael Borland, please," Cheryl said. The receptionist couldn't be more than a size two, and she wore a loose shirt that draped over her thin frame and white skinny jeans. Cheryl suddenly felt dowdy in her blouse and slacks.

"Do you have an appointment?" Dangly earrings danced as she moved.

"No, but I was hoping he could spare a few minutes," Cheryl said and gave what she hoped was an endearing smile.

The woman looked at her with thinly veiled disdain. Cheryl heard voices and footsteps in the back, behind the door that led to the rear part of the office, but it was just Cheryl and the receptionist out here.

"I'm afraid he doesn't see anyone without an appointment."

"In that case, do you know when he might have a free appointment?"

The woman studied her. "He is a very busy man."

Well. Cheryl could see she wasn't going to get anywhere this way, so she decided to try another tactic.

"I can just sit here and wait until he has a moment," Cheryl said, a bit too brightly. She moved toward one of the chairs on the far side of the waiting room, a midcentury design covered in white leather. Cheryl sat down and dug her book out of her purse.

"Can you tell me what this is in regard to? I'll ask him when he's free," the woman said.

"It's about a piece of land he's made an offer on over in Sugarcreek," Cheryl answered, smiling. She opened the book and took out the sticky note she was using as a bookmark.

The woman rolled her eyes, and then she sighed, pushed herself up, and walked toward the door that opened to the back. She teetered on heels that had to be at least three inches high. "One moment please."

Once the receptionist had disappeared, Cheryl looked around the waiting area a bit more carefully. On the wall closest to the door, there was a framed diploma. She squinted and saw that it was from Dartmouth, which she knew was an elite college in the

Northeast. The name Michael Borland was scrawled in a heavy script. Well. Dartmouth was a good school and all, but to Cheryl it seemed a teensy bit pretentious to hang your Ivy League diploma right there in the waiting room. Unless you really wanted to project a certain kind of image, Cheryl supposed. She could imagine what Naomi would think—that the man had *hochmut*, or pride.

Cheryl continued looking around the room and noticed that the black-and-white photographs she'd seen before were pictures of shopping centers and office buildings. That was an odd choice. Cheryl usually preferred more scenic work—landscapes, still lifes, that kind of thing. He did seem to be into modern décor, though, so maybe these were the new hot thing. She looked at one and noticed that the picture of the shopping center had a sign by the entrance that said Hunter Pointe Center.

Now that she looked at it, it didn't look like an artistic photo so much as a real place. Could these photos be...?

Cheryl pulled out her phone and used the Internet to search for the named Hunter Pointe Center, as well as the term "developer."

Sure enough, the first result was an article in the local paper, the Canton *Repository*, which mentioned the shopping center and its builder, Michael Borland. Were these photos all pictures of the developments Michael's company had worked on?

But wait—Cheryl skimmed the rest of the article. What was this? The article was about delays and problems with the construction of the shopping center. It seemed the planned shopping center had cost several million dollars more than anticipated and had taken more than a year longer than it should have, mostly because of local lawsuits filed on behalf of neighboring landowners, who claimed that the land for the shopping center had been obtained illegally. But one line especially chilled her: "Borland's company has faced a string of lawsuits in recent years and has developed something of a reputation for preying on Amish farmers, who are less likely to bring a lawsuit, in his quest to develop the Ohio countryside."

So he'd done this before? Cheryl reread the article a bit more carefully, and yes, the article did seem to suggest that Borland Developers had a reputation for taking land from Amish farmers through marginally legal—or not legal at all—means. How could she find out more?

"Miss Cooper?"

Cheryl looked up and saw the receptionist had returned.

"I'm afraid Mr. Borland is out of the office at the moment," she said, though the look on her face made it clear she wasn't at all sorry.

"Oh." Out of the office? Why hadn't she said so before? It seemed like she might have mentioned that at some point before this. It certainly was suspicious, Cheryl thought. "Do you know when he might be back?"

"I'm afraid I don't." She sat down in her chair and turned to her computer.

"Can I leave a message for him to give me a call?" Cheryl asked.

The woman hesitated, and then she sighed. "I will try to get it to him."

Cheryl wanted her to do more than try, but knew she couldn't say that. Again, more flies with honey and all that.

Cheryl left her name and phone number as well as her e-mail address, and the woman nodded, wrote them down, and turned back to her computer screen.

Cheryl turned and headed back down the elevator and out the glass door of the building. But as she headed to her car, she noticed something in the parking lot. A sleek black sports car with a vanity license plate that said MikeyB. With a Dartmouth sticker on the back windshield.

That had to be his car.

Which meant that Michael Borland was here, at the office. The receptionist had lied to her. But why? It was obvious she had wanted Cheryl to leave, but was it simply because Michael was, as the receptionist had put it, a very busy man?

Cheryl believed that was true, but she also couldn't help but wonder at the change that had occurred once Cheryl had said why she was there. Before she'd told the receptionist she was asking about Silas's land, she had said she would ask when Michael would be free. After the announcement, she had said he wasn't there at all. Was it because he hadn't wanted to talk about that land that she'd changed her tune?

Cheryl thought about it all the way back to Sugarcreek. There was no way to say for sure, but she did know one thing, and that was that she needed to talk to Michael Borland, as soon as possible. She would need to find a way to get him to talk to her.

As she got back to the outskirts of Sugarcreek, Cheryl's mind shifted gears, and she thought about the idea she'd hatched after her visit to the Honey Bee earlier. She decided to make a few stops before she headed back to the Swiss Miss. She had already been gone for quite a while this afternoon, but she knew that Lydia Troyer was scheduled to be in the shop all afternoon and was perfectly capable of handling the crowds.

Cheryl started at Artistic License, a small art studio and gallery located in the same building as the Honey Bee. After a quick chat with Roxanna Velandria, who owned the shop, she ducked into By His Grace, a Christian bookstore just down from her own shop, and talked with Marion Berryhill, who quickly agreed to her idea. Then she ducked into Buttons 'n Bows, Yoder's Corner—where Greta Yoder was getting things ready for the early dinner rush— and to Hoffman's Furniture and was very pleased by the enthusiastic response she received. Then, finally, Cheryl headed back to the Swiss Miss.

"Goodness. It looks like you've had quite a day," Cheryl said as she stepped inside. Lydia looked up from the display of handmade soaps and lotions and smiled.

"A busload came in a little while ago. Thankfully, it was just before Esther had to go home, so she was able to help. But"—she gestured at the depleted display—"I am just now getting a chance to refill the shelves. That must be the cleanest, best-smelling bus in history."

Cheryl laughed. It was funny how certain groups of tourists seemed to buy certain things. Once she'd had a group from

Michigan completely wipe her out of hand-carved chess sets; something she only sold a few of per month regularly.

"I'm sorry I was gone for so long," Cheryl said.

"That is okay. I do not mind." Lydia stacked a bar of rose-scented soap on a lavender bar and arranged it carefully. "The women were nice, and they did not mind waiting as I rang them up. In fact, I am sure we sold more of that candy"—she gestured at the jars of bright penny candy near the register—"as they kept adding more to their baskets while they waited."

Cheryl smiled. Back in Columbus, she might have gotten frustrated if she'd had to wait more than five minutes for anything, but life seemed to move at a slower pace here, and she knew that even if the tourists had had to wait for a little while, being served by real Amish girls made it worthwhile for the customers. And, except for the soaps and lotions, everything looked pretty well stocked. Cheryl took a few minutes to set out some more homemade fudge as well as some of the jars of jam she'd gotten from Naomi the night before, and then she went back behind the counter, took a piece of paper out of the store's printer, and set about making up a schedule. She would go back and show it to Kathy Snyder at the Honey Bee after she closed up shop for the day, and she hoped Kathy would be pleased.

Then she thought back over her conversation with Seth and Levi on the car ride back to the Miller farm. She needed to wait for Naomi's help to get in contact with the Amish cleaning girl and for Seth to check with the Amish man, Henry King, who had owned the land before the Englisher who sold it to Silas. But there was one name that had come up that she could learn more about. She pulled out the phone book for Sugarcreek and turned to the heading for lawyers. As she suspected, there it was: a listing for Luke Bradshaw, Attorney at Law, out on Thistle Hill Road.

Cheryl was tempted to hop in her car and drive out there now, but it was almost five o'clock, and she had to catch Kathy Snyder before she closed the café. And she didn't want a repeat of what had happened at the developer's office.

Instead, she dialed the number, and an older woman with a raspy voice said Luke Bradshaw could see her the next afternoon. Cheryl tried to insist that she didn't need legal advice, she just wanted to ask him a few questions, but the woman insisted she would need to come to the office to do so. Cheryl thanked her, marked the appointment in her calendar, and put the phone book back. She sure hoped she would be able to talk to him without being charged a lawyer's fee. She'd worry about that later.

Lydia walked back to the rear of the shop, carrying an empty cardboard box. "You will probably need to order more soap," Lydia said. Cheryl nodded and said she would be in touch with Anna Byler soon.

"Thank you for your help today. I really appreciate it," Cheryl said as Lydia set the box down by the back door and lifted off her apron. "And you're still okay with opening the store tomorrow?" Cheryl had run her idea past Lydia earlier, and, like the capable Amish girl she was, she simply nodded and said it would not be a problem to open up the store while Cheryl put her plan to help Kathy in motion.

"It will be fine." Lydia had slung her purse over her shoulder and had already pulled her cell phone out. Like most teenagers, Amish or not, Lydia was obsessed with her phone. "I will see you tomorrow."

"See you then," she called and watched as Lydia waved, threaded her way through the shop, and stepped out the front door. Cheryl closed out the register, turned off the computer, shut off the lights, and locked the front door of the shop. She hurried across the street to the Honey Bee and was glad to see it had quieted down since this afternoon.

"Hi, Cheryl. Back again?" Kathy was wiping down the counter with a clean rag. "Can I interest you in some cookies? They're half price." She gestured toward the dessert case. "I'm trying to clean everything out so it doesn't go bad while I'm away."

"Actually, I wanted to talk to you about that," Cheryl said. "I was thinking what a shame it was that you had to close during one of the busiest times of the year. I assume that you, like most of us, rely on the income from these summer months to make it through the rest of the year."

"It is bad timing, for sure," Kathy said. "I sure wish Bella hadn't quit last week. With Heather away, I just don't know what else to do."

"What would you say if I told you I had an idea for how you could stay open this week?"

Kathy stopped wiping the counter and looked at Cheryl. "What do you mean?"

"I talked with some of the other store owners, and we want to help. We'll take turns covering the café. I drew up a schedule"—

Cheryl reached into her purse and pulled out the calendar she'd drawn up earlier—"and I think we're going to be able to cover you the whole time you're gone."

Kathy dropped the rag and put her hands to her mouth. "Are you for real?"

"We're willing to give it a shot, anyway. I know we probably won't do as good a job as you usually do, and for the most part there will only be one of us at a time, so the customers may have to deal with slower service than normal. But if you show me what needs to be done, I can teach the others, and we should be able to keep things running. I'll open up and clean up every night."

Kathy shook her head. "You're serious, aren't you?"

"I really am."

"I don't know what to say."

"Well, you could start by showing me how to work that fancy espresso machine you've got there," Cheryl said.

Kathy watched her. "Are you sure? All these people are really willing to give up time at their own businesses to come here and help me?"

"Why wouldn't they? You are such a beloved part of this community. Everyone jumped at the chance to thank you for all you do for us." Cheryl started to move around the counter to the back. "Besides, it's only for a few days. How much trouble can we get into in a few days?"

Kathy still looked like she couldn't believe it, but she started demonstrating how to load the espresso powder and use the milk frother. Cheryl took copious notes as Kathy explained which breads and rolls were delivered and which items in the dessert case were made from scratch. She showed Cheryl where the recipes were, and Cheryl assured her that the Amish women who had volunteered to help would make short work of any baking. Then when they had gone over everything either one of them could think of, Kathy handed over the keys.

"Are you *sure* you're up for this?" Kathy asked, giving Cheryl one last chance to back out.

"I am positive. Your customers won't even know you're gone."

Kathy laughed. "I hope they at least miss me a little."

"Fine," Cheryl said. "Just a little. But don't worry. Your shop will be in good hands."

CHAPTER FIVE

The next morning dawned overcast but very warm. It was going to be a scorcher, Cheryl could already tell the moment she stepped out of bed—and the sun was barely up yet. Even with the window unit air conditioner on full blast, her bedroom was sticky and still. Beau, her Siamese cat, wanted to snuggle, but Cheryl just patted him on the head, wary of holding his warm body so close to hers. She quickly dressed in a light summer dress, got herself ready, and headed over to Main Street. The sun was still casting long shadows as she parked in front of the Honey Bee.

The first thing Cheryl did when she stepped inside the café was to brew a pot of coffee. She didn't know how Kathy could wake up this early every day. Then as the rich earthy aroma of coffee started to fill the air inside the café, Cheryl turned to the list of tasks she needed to do before opening the doors for the day. There should be a delivery of rolls and bread coming, she knew, but the muffins and scones needed to be made from scratch.

Cheryl looked around. Where had Kathy said she would find the recipes for those? Cheryl couldn't remember. She checked in all the drawers under the counter, in the kitchen in the back, and inside the small office at the rear of the store. Nothing. Well, maybe Cheryl could Google something similar. She knew where

Kathy kept the baking supplies, and after she pulled up a recipe for chocolate chip scones she'd found online, she started measuring out her ingredients.

Actually, this wasn't so bad, Cheryl thought. Baking wasn't exactly her specialty, but she was improving lately, and she could follow a recipe. It was kind of nice to spend the morning baking—peaceful and quiet, with just herself, her coffee, and her thoughts. Cheryl prayed while she shaped and cut the dough, asking God to help her find answers about Levi's land and for protection and comfort for Seth's family, who would be traveling today to be in town for the funeral. Then she slid the scones into the oven, washed the dishes, and started working on a batch of peach crumble muffins.

Soon it was time for her to open the café, and she unlocked the doors and stood behind the counter. When her first customer of the day came in, Cheryl greeted her warmly and poured her a cup of coffee to go and handed her a still-warm scone.

"Is there milk and sugar?" the woman asked, lifting the pitcher that was supposed to contain whole milk. Containers for a variety of different types of sugars were lined up on a small shelf near the trash cans, and Cheryl realized she needed to top those off.

"Oh! I forgot to fill those," Cheryl said. "Hang on."

She pulled the jug of milk out of the industrial fridge and saw that she was running low on skim milk. She'd need to run out at some point and get some more. She filled the whole milk jug and did her best with the skim, and by the time she'd poured the half and half and added packets of sugar, she had a line waiting at the counter.

"Do you have any of those yummy croissants?" a woman Cheryl vaguely recognized asked. Cheryl thought she worked part-time at Amazin' Corn, a corn maze run by Bob and Tillie Gleason that was popular with tourists.

"Oh goodness." What had Kathy said about those? Were those supposed to come with the bread order? Speaking of which… Cheryl craned her neck and saw that the bread had been left in a bag that was hung from the doorknob of the front door.

"Hang on one moment," Cheryl said, and she ran over to grab the bag and looked through it. She saw rolls, buns, and bread for sandwiches, but no croissants. "I'm sorry, I don't think we have those today," she said breathlessly, eyeing the line of customers. Some were shifting from foot to foot.

"I'll just take one of those muffins," the woman said, "and a large cappuccino to go."

"Coming right up." Cheryl used bakery paper to pull the muffin out of the case and set it in a bag, and then she turned to the espresso machine. Okay. She knew how to do this. She poured espresso powder into the filter, tamped it down, and started the machine. Rich dark liquid spilled out. Then she poured milk into the jug and used the metal arm to froth it. Finally, she poured the milk into the cup and added the espresso. Cheryl knew she'd at least gotten this part right. When she turned and handed it to the woman, she smiled, but then she couldn't find the right square on the touch-screen register to ring up the drink. The woman let out a pronounced sigh, and Cheryl noticed that the line now stretched to the door. One man toward the back of the line gave up and left.

Cheryl wasn't sure how Kathy did this every day. Sure, she usually had help, and it probably got easier once you were more comfortable with it. Kathy was always so pleasant and cheerful, but this was way harder than it looked.

Cheryl did her best to get through the line and serve the customers quickly and pleasantly, but she couldn't have been more grateful when Marion Berryhill came in to relieve her.

"Thank you." Cheryl tried not to sound too desperate as she wiped her hands and took off the white apron she'd been wearing.

"No problem. I'm glad to help Kathy. Now show me what needs to be done." Marion was a tall, gorgeous African-American woman with a calming, capable presence. Marion and her husband Ray had been surprised—and thrilled—when they found out Marion was pregnant last year, and now their little daughter Eden was a common presence in their bookstore and a local celebrity.

Cheryl went over the list of things Kathy had told her needed to happen to prepare for lunch and showed her how to make drinks and use the register. Just before she left, she tried to give Marion a bit of a warning.

"This was more difficult than I expected. I don't know how Kathy does it. Just do your best."

Marion waved her concerns away. "I survived having a newborn. Nothing seems scary or hard to me anymore."

Cheryl laughed, reminded Marion to call if she needed anything, and then stepped out the door into the brilliant June sunshine. It was hot all right, just as the dawn had promised.

Cheryl hurried quickly across Route 39 and into the Swiss Miss, where Lydia had the air-conditioning blasting. It felt glorious.

Cheryl quickly saw that there were a handful of customers browsing, and Lydia was ringing up one woman buying a stack of quilted pot holders, but Lydia really did have everything under control. The difference between this scene and the one she'd just left was astounding. Cheryl thanked God for Lydia, and then she headed to the back room and dropped off her purse and slipped on an apron.

"Thank you," Cheryl said after Lydia had finished ringing up her customer. "Everything looks great in here. Have you been busy?"

"About the same as usual." Lydia shrugged. "A busload came in right at ten, but they were very nice. It was not hard."

Now, more than ever before, Cheryl appreciated exactly how hard it was to manage a crowded shop, and once again she was thankful for Lydia. And then, without being asked, Lydia ceded the counter to Cheryl and went out to the floor to see if any of the customers needed help.

Cheryl looked around to see what needed to be done around the shop, but, really, things looked good. The displays were fully stocked, and everything looked neat and tidy. Cheryl decided that it would be a good time to make a phone call.

Cheryl pulled up the picture of the business card for Michael Borland she'd taken yesterday and dialed the number. She held her breath, but the phone rang and rang, and finally she was dumped into voice mail.

That was strange. It was just past eleven o'clock—firmly during business hours. She tried the number again, but this time her call was directed straight to voice mail. She didn't get the impression an operation like Borland Developers was lackadaisical about answering their phones. Could it be...? Cheryl had left her number with the receptionist. Most businesses these days had phones with caller ID built in. Could the woman at the front desk be ignoring Cheryl's calls?

Cheryl didn't know what to think, but she tried once more and then gave up. She would find a way to speak to Michael Borland.

In the meantime, she wanted to know more about this Michael Borland character. She did an Internet search and came across a social media profile, but it was restricted to his friends. All she could see was that he'd gone to Dartmouth, which she already knew, and that he worked at Borland Developers, which she'd also gathered. She studied the little profile picture. It showed a man in his early to midthirties, she guessed, standing on a beach in some tropical locale. He wasn't bad looking, she realized. Square jaw, dark full hair, big brown eyes. She scanned the list of his friends, but she didn't have a connection to any of them. There wasn't more she could learn here, she decided, so she clicked back to the search page to see what else had turned up. A LinkedIn profile, a phone number lookup page...and then, what was this? This could be something.

Cheryl clicked on a link and was taken to what looked like a page from an Ohio State Business School alumni magazine. It was a profile of Michael, and the accompanying picture showed the same man she'd seen on the social media page, but this time he was dressed in a suit and tie. Cheryl skimmed the article and saw that he had grown up in a hoity-toity area of Columbus, one Cheryl couldn't have afforded in her dreams, and had summered on Nantucket. According to the article, after going "back East" for college, he'd returned to Ohio for business school because "people here are real, they're genuine. You don't see too much of that in the Ivy League."

Cheryl had to restrain herself from laughing. She fought hard to concentrate and read on. The article said Michael had taken over Borland Developers from his father, Michael Borland Sr., who had started the business thirty years ago. Michael Borland Jr. had made big changes in the company in the five years since he'd taken over, she read. He'd been aggressive with acquisitions and proposals and had won several key projects, even though larger, more established companies had bid for them as well.

The article made it seem like he was a huge success story for the school. And maybe he was. But Cheryl couldn't help wondering how many people he had pushed out of the way to get there.

She clicked back to the search page and scanned the rest of the results, but none of them yielded any new information. She sat back and tried to think of what to do next.

The article she'd read earlier had said that his previous deals had taken advantage of the Amish. How could she find out more? Cheryl found the article she'd come across before and reread it. It referenced several lawsuits filed against him. She wondered where she could find out more about those. She tried searching online and came up with abstracts for a couple articles, but the full articles weren't available online unless she was a subscriber. Huh. Well, Cheryl wasn't a subscriber to the Canton *Repository*. But she did know who was.

Cheryl looked up as a tour bus rolled up in front of the shop. She couldn't leave Lydia again, not now. But—she checked the clock—yes, the Sugarcreek Library should be open. Cheryl looked up the number for the library and called. She spoke with Pam, a friendly librarian who had helped her find information in the past, and explained that she was looking for articles about lawsuits involving Borland Developers in back issues of the Canton *Repository.*

"*Ooh*, sounds fun," Pam said. "I'll see what I can find."

"I really appreciate your help," Cheryl said.

"I appreciate the excuse to stop reshelving children's books. I love research, so this is right up my alley."

Cheryl was glad there were people like Pam in the world. Pam had an advanced degree in library science and had worked in libraries her whole career, and she always seemed genuinely interested in digging through old files and squinting at blurry microfiche screens.

"I'll let you know what I find," Pam promised, sounding much more cheerful than she had when she'd picked up the phone. Cheryl chuckled and put down the phone, then she readied herself to focus on the task at hand. Within a few minutes, the shop was filled with older women in matching T-shirts, and Cheryl had a good time helping them find souvenirs for their grandchildren and husbands. A steady stream of customers kept her focused, and she didn't even realize the shop was emptying out until she looked up and saw Jessica Stockton threading her way through the displays toward the counter.

"Hello, Jessica," Cheryl said, smiling at the woman. "Thank you so much for your help with the Millers. I'm told you were the one who let them know someone was trying to buy the land from under them."

Jessica nodded to acknowledge her words. "Hi, Cheryl." Jessica's voice was deep, and she was direct and could come off as a bit gruff, but she was a sweet woman who enjoyed getting to know the Amish she drove. "I just dropped off a load of women at The Old Amish Store, and I'm glad I am nearby because I just got a call from Jeff and he has more news."

"Oh?" Cheryl felt her heartbeat race. Could they have found the title? Maybe Jeff had been calling to say it had all been a big misunderstanding and that the land was Levi's free and clear. But one look at Jessica's face crushed those hopes.

"Something strange is going on. Jeff called to let me know that the closing for the sale of the land has been scheduled for Friday. I wanted to let you know right away."

"Friday? As in, *this* Friday?" Cheryl's stomach dropped. That was in two days.

Jessica nodded. "At three."

"But…" She struggled to find words. "How is that possible?"

"I don't know. It shouldn't be possible, not if there's question about who really owns the land. Jeff thinks that developer must have some friends in high places at the courthouse who are pushing this all through." Jessica pressed her lips together and then added, "No doubt friends in some high places who are suddenly a little bit richer."

Cheryl understood the implication. After what she'd read online, she thought it was pretty likely that Borland Developers had cash to throw around to help, well, make things move quickly.

"I can't believe it," Cheryl said, shaking her head.

Except that she could believe it. She could imagine it all too well.

"One more thing. Jeff thinks there's a reason, besides money, that the government is moving things along so quickly."

"What is it?"

"Development plans were submitted just this morning for Jeff's office to approve. They want to build a prison on that piece of land."

"A *prison*?" Cheryl tried to take that in.

"A small one. Minimum security. But a prison, at any rate. Apparently, it's something the county has been looking to do for a while, to relieve overcrowding at other facilities, and this developer had plans drawn up that others in Jeff's department approve of. For whatever reason, this is seen as the perfect plot of land for this project. Which means that if he gets the land, he gets the contract to build it."

Cheryl still couldn't believe it. The thought of a shopping center or condos had been bad enough, but a prison? She knew the whole community would be against the idea of a prison in their midst. Which, Cheryl realized now, was probably the point. If the community at large knew that a prison was in the works, there would no doubt be widespread protests. Besides being an eyesore, having a prison nearby would mean unsavory people just a few fences away as well as increased traffic in the area. Cheryl had heard of this sort of thing happening other places—when she'd lived in Columbus, in fact, a new parole center in her neighborhood had been quietly approved by the city before anyone in the community got wind of it. Once it came out, several community groups sued and eventually managed to block it, but just barely. It sounded like something similar was happening here. The county was probably just as eager for Borland Developers to break ground as Michael Borland was to get the contract.

"How can we stop this?" Cheryl asked.

"My first suggestion is to lawyer up," Jessica said. Cheryl nodded. Seth hadn't given her an answer about hiring a lawyer yet. Maybe if they realized it was not just their family who would be at risk if they couldn't prove their claim on the land, they would be more willing.

"And I'm thinking I might call my sister-in-law. She works over at the *Times-Reporter*, in circulation, but I bet she could put me in touch with a reporter who would be interested in hearing about how the county is rushing through a sale so they can build a jail before the community has a chance to have a say about it."

"Oh, would you? That would be amazing."

Jessica nodded. "I'll give her a call as soon as I leave here. Okay if I tell them to contact you?"

"That's just fine," Cheryl said.

"Will do. In the meantime, the best thing you can do is to find that deed."

"We're trying, but I will definitely try harder," Cheryl said. Goodness. She *really* needed to help Levi find it now.

"I'm sorry to come in here and dump all this on you," Jessica said, but Cheryl shook her head.

"Thank you so much. Without your help, we wouldn't have known about any of this. I'm going to do what I can to help stop this."

"Well, let me know if there's anything I can do. I hate the thought of anyone taking advantage of an Amish family, and I'm afraid that's what's going on here."

Cheryl thought for a moment. They needed to find Silas's copy of the deed, but also, as she'd already pointed out, there should have been one filed with the county, both in the paper files and in the electronic database. The fact that there wasn't was highly suspect. What she needed was a way to figure out who might possibly have had the opportunity to remove those.

"Jessica, do you know if the county keeps records of who accesses the property records files?" she asked.

"I see what you're getting at. And I don't know, but I can ask Jeff." She thought for a minute and nodded. "They must have some sort of records for that." Just then, a timer went off on her phone. "Whoops, that's my cue to head back to the van. I need to go."

"Thank you so much for your help," Cheryl said, and Jessica waved and headed toward the door.

"No problem. And I'll let you know what Jeff says about those records."

"Thanks!"

Jessica disappeared out the door, and Cheryl looked around and saw that Lydia was helping a mother with young children pick out some candy from the penny jars.

There were a few customers browsing the hand-carved whistles and toys. Cheryl was just about to see if they needed help when the bell over the door dinged, and she looked up to see Naomi Miller and Esther step into the shop.

"Naomi." Cheryl couldn't help but smile at the sight of her dear friend. Naomi was so busy at the farm these days that she didn't get into town as much as she would have liked, and Cheryl was thrilled to see her. "How are you?"

"I am all right," Naomi said. She gave a smile, but the lines around her eyes gave away her fatigue. "I am preparing for the visitation later today and the funeral tomorrow, which means much running around."

"Yikes. I'm sorry." Until Cheryl's grandfather had died, she'd had no idea there were so many models of caskets with so many features. And of course, there were the questions of which hymns and scriptures to read, what flowers to choose, and who would lead the service: Cheryl's father, who was a pastor, or the pastor of her grandfather's church. And then there had been the food after the service to worry about. She thought the process of planning the funeral had been almost as hard for her father as losing his dad.

"Is there anything I can do to help? I know more about the features of various caskets than anyone should."

Naomi tilted her head and gave her a strange look. "Seth has already built a pine box for his brother. What features should it have?"

Cheryl smiled. "Never mind." Now that she thought about it, it made sense that the Amish would simply bury their loved ones in pine boxes. Debating between velvet versus satin lining was not something her Amish friends—who sat on backless wooden benches through three-hour church services—would have any patience for. They were plain in life, why not in death? "So have you been to Sugarcreek Florist down the road?"

Again, Naomi cocked her head. "What do you mean?"

"You guys don't do flowers at funerals?"

"I am sorry, Cheryl. Our funerals must be very different from yours." Naomi smiled. "I have gone to the market to buy more flour and such, and then I have been visiting the Amish merchants here in town to make sure they know about the visitation and funeral."

"Ah." Cheryl guessed she shouldn't have been surprised. Among the Amish, word had to travel mostly by mouth. "Is there anything I can do to help?"

"Yes." Naomi nodded and perked up a bit. "You can come with me to see Ruthanna Yutzy. Seth told me you needed to meet with her. I need to speak with her mother anyway, and I have some time this morning. I will take you there now."

It took Cheryl a minute to catch up, but then she remembered that Ruthanna was the Amish girl who cleaned Silas's home. She was the one whose name Seth and Levi had been reluctant to tell her.

"That would be great." Cheryl started to untie her apron but then paused. "You're sure now is an okay time? You've got a lot going on."

"Of course." Naomi looked at her like she didn't understand. And Cheryl should have known by now not to question her friend. Naomi wouldn't have suggested it if this wasn't a good time.

"I'll be ready in just a moment," Cheryl said. Esther had emerged from the back wearing her red apron, and Cheryl told her and Lydia she was stepping out. Both girls nodded and said good-bye.

A minute later, Cheryl slid behind the wheel of her car, and Naomi was settling in beside her. Cheryl, following Naomi's directions, pulled out on to Route 39. Soon they were past the small downtown and surrounded by cornfields.

"What is that noise?" Naomi's brow wrinkled.

"What noise?"

"That whining sound."

"Oh, that." Cheryl laughed. "Your husband and son mentioned that yesterday too. It's fine. I hardly even notice it. But I'll take it in to get it looked at."

"I hope you will do so soon."

Cheryl nodded and tried to figure out how much of what she knew to tell Naomi. She hesitated to bring up what she'd learned from Jessica Stockton—Naomi was already dealing with so much—and yet she knew her friend needed to know.

"Jessica Stockton stopped by this morning," Cheryl said.

"Oh yes?" Naomi turned her head to see Cheryl better.

"She told me that the closing date for the land has been set for Friday."

Naomi didn't respond right away, and Cheryl wasn't sure what to do, so she continued.

"It seems really fast, too fast, and Jessica thinks the developer must have friends in high places and to have issued some bribes. Which means we don't have much time. She suggested getting a lawyer and so did Chief Twitchell, and at this point I think it's probably a good idea. We need someone to try to block the sale from going through until we can prove the land belonged to Silas."

Naomi nodded, gently, so Cheryl could tell she had heard, but she didn't respond the way Cheryl would have—with anger, frustration, and fear. Instead, Naomi simply said, "I will talk to Seth about it."

Cheryl wasn't sure her friend understood the gravity of the situation. "If we don't find that deed, we need to find some way to block the sale, otherwise the land will be sold off on Friday. Levi will lose the land Silas left him."

Naomi nodded again. "Yes, I understand. I will talk to Seth about it."

"Jessica also told me that the land will be developed into a jail facility."

"Goodness." Naomi crinkled up her nose. "I do hope not."

"That's why I really think it would be best if you…"

Naomi nodded. "I will talk to Seth. I do not know what he will want to do until I have a chance to talk to him." She gestured toward an intersection coming up. "Turn left up here."

"Are you serious?" Cheryl glanced at her friend, trying to figure out what she was thinking.

"Yes, I am very serious. This is where you need to turn." Naomi gave her a sly grin.

"How can you be so calm? Someone is trying to take away the land that should belong to your stepson, and through shady means. How can you be so laid-back about it?"

Naomi didn't answer for a moment, and then, carefully, she said, "I do not worry about it because it is in *Gott's* hands."

Cheryl felt a wave of shame wash over her. Of course it was. How had she forgotten that? Her first reaction was to get angry and worked up, but her Amish friend's calm, quiet certainty that God was in control was humbling.

"I think it is partly because I have been spending so much time preparing for a funeral that I have been reminded that none of this really matters anyway," Naomi went on. "Silas was a good man, a humble man who loved the Lord and served his church. That is all that matters now."

That was also true, Cheryl knew. In the face of death, things like acreage didn't really matter all that much. It was just dirt, ultimately.

And yet…

While Cheryl did agree with what Naomi was saying—that, as bumper stickers put it so glibly, you can't take it with you—did that mean that you shouldn't stand up for what was yours here on earth?

"But Silas owned that land. It's valuable property, and Levi is your husband's son. Why would you *not* stand up for him?"

Once again Naomi stopped to think before she spoke, and then she said, "I love Levi like he is one of my own. Of course I want him to get the land his uncle left for him. I wish for him to have a home and farm of his own someday." She turned her head and gazed out at the cornfields as they passed. "But more than that, I want him to trust in the Lord to provide. And if that means losing that land, then so be it. If that land is not for Levi, I know that Gott has something better in store for him."

Cheryl didn't know what to say. As a preacher's kid and someone who went to church regularly, she often thought she had all the answers. But so often her Amish friend showed her what true, deep faith looked like, and she was humbled all over again.

"Of course, I would still like for you to find that deed," Naomi said and looked at her with a smile.

"I will try," Cheryl said. "The locksmith is coming in a couple hours to try to get the safe opened."

"I hope he is successful."

"I do too." Cheryl thought through what Naomi had recently shared. "But I will try to remember God is in control no matter what."

"Good then." Naomi nodded. "And just in time, since Ruthanna lives just up there."

Cheryl slowed and put on her blinker, and then she turned into the driveway that led up to a neat two-story home. There was a wide front porch and a carefully tended flower garden.

"Ruthanna's husband, Daniel, works for his father's cabinetry business," Naomi said, nodding at the house. "They do quite well, so they have this big house and it is only the two of them who live in it, though Ruthanna's mother is often here visiting." She pressed her lips together and then said, "I think she enjoys coming here because this house is nicer than her own."

It was the closest Naomi came to gossip, but Cheryl appreciated the context. So Ruthanna was married but had no children, and her husband's family was well-off. In a typical English house, she would have expected to see European sports cars or pools and outbuildings as evidence of wealth, but she did not know what status symbols looked like for the Amish. Probably they did not encourage such things.

"Have they been married long?" Cheryl knew that most Amish women were anxious to start having a family once they were married, but perhaps it hadn't been all that long.

"Nearly a year," Naomi said. She stepped out of the car. "Though Ruthanna is a bit older. Nearly twenty-four, I believe. She took many classes at the college and took quite a long time to decide whether to join the church or not."

Naomi closed the car door and indicated that Cheryl should follow her. Cheryl tried not to care that twenty-four was considered old for marriage in the Amish world. At thirty-one, Cheryl would no doubt be considered an old maid.

"But she did decide to join in the end," Cheryl said.

"Yes, she did. She married Daniel Yutzy, who had always had a crush on her. He eventually won her over. It was very sweet." Naomi walked up the steps. "It was a very nice wedding. So much joy."

She rang the doorbell, and as it echoed through the house, Cheryl thought about what Naomi had said. Ruthanna had taken college-level classes. That really was an accomplishment, as most Amish were only educated through eighth grade. She must have continued her education in an English high school or gotten a GED and then enrolled in college classes. Not many Amish parents encouraged or allowed such things, and she admired the girl's ambition.

The door was pulled open, and a tall, willowy girl with dark hair and deep blue eyes stood in the doorway. "*Guder mariye*, Naomi," Ruthanna said, smiling first at her and then at Cheryl. She wore a kapp and apron with her long, dark green dress. Ruthanna was startlingly pretty, and she had a gentle voice, and you could see in her eyes that there was a spark in her. "Please, come inside."

"Hi, Ruthanna. This is my friend Cheryl," Naomi said and then followed up with something in Pennsylvania Dutch. Ruthanna's smile widened, and she gestured for them to follow her inside. Her skirt and apron swished as she led them down a hallway and past a large kitchen, where an Amish woman sat at the table shelling peas into a bowl.

Ruthanna paused in the doorway. "Maam, *kommen sie mit?*"

Naomi greeted the woman, and the older woman replied in their language. The women chatted for a few minutes, and then Ruthanna nodded and started walking again, leading them into a wide sitting room. Naomi caught her eye, as if pointing out that she was right, but Cheryl still wasn't exactly sure which were the signs of the family's wealth. It kind of looked like every other Amish home she'd ever been inside.

"*Es dutt mir leed.* My mother was helping me gather vegetables from the garden earlier, and she would like to keep working on the peas. She wishes that you please forgive her," Ruthanna said to both Naomi and Cheryl, and Cheryl nodded.

"That is just fine," Naomi said. "'Pride in your work puts joy in your day.' That is a proverb my mother was very fond of using."

"Thank you for taking the time to talk with us," Cheryl said. They'd dropped by uninvited, with no warning. She hardly expected the woman to drop everything and come talk to a stranger, and she was thankful Ruthanna had done so.

"It is my pleasure. Please, sit," Ruthanna said, gesturing toward two chairs. "Would you like some *kaffee*? And I have strawberry pie."

It was just around lunchtime, and Cheryl hadn't eaten since early this morning. Her stomach rumbled at the thought.

"Pie sounds lovely," Cheryl said. "And I never turn down coffee."

"Make that two," Naomi said. Ruthanna said she would be right back, and Naomi caught Cheryl's eye again and looked around the room. Cheryl smiled but made a note to ask Naomi later what it was that showed how well-off this family was. She really couldn't see it.

Ruthanna returned with two plates of pie and set them down on the wooden coffee table and then came back a moment later with two cups of strong dark coffee as well as a small pitcher of cream and a bowl of sugar. Cheryl noted that the dishes were finely made porcelain, not the cheaper ceramic that so many people—including herself—used for everyday tableware, but the dishes were still plain white. Was this what Amish showiness looked like? She picked up the cream jug and watched it swirl into the rich dark brew. Cheryl wouldn't have even noticed the difference if she hadn't started doing research on items for her registry before Lance broke off their engagement. She dumped in a spoonful of sugar and stirred.

"I am sure you heard my husband's brother Silas passed on earlier this week," Naomi said.

Ruthanna nodded. Cheryl noticed that she hadn't served herself a slice of pie and that she took her coffee with just a splash of cream. That must be how she stayed so thin.

"I did. Silas was a wonderful man, and he was always very fair to me. I will miss him."

"How long did you work for him?" Naomi asked.

"Oh, let's see." Ruthanna pressed her back against the spindles of her chair. "It must have been . . . Goodness. Three years, maybe. I started after his wife passed on."

"How often did you clean for him?" Naomi asked. She picked up her fork and cut off a bite of her pie, so Cheryl did the same.

"Twice a week," Ruthanna said and then took a sip from her cup. "And I cooked for him one afternoon a week. It was not enough to feed him the full week, but it was enough to ensure that he did not starve." She looked at Cheryl over the rim of her cup and lifted an eyebrow. "Which I sometimes thought he might otherwise."

"Silas was often distracted," Naomi said, nodding. "And he always said he enjoyed your cooking. You took good care of him."

"I tried."

"When was the last time you cleaned for him?" Cheryl asked. Ruthanna looked at Naomi, who nodded, and then she answered.

"Last week. I was scheduled to go yesterday, but, well..."

Cheryl nodded, indicating that she understood. Then she raised the fork to her mouth. Whoa. This pie was delicious. There was a dusting of granulated sugar on the crust and it added such an unexpected sweet crunch.

"Cheryl is helping us try to locate the deed for Silas's land," Naomi said. "The section with the alfalfa fields. It is missing, and we need to find it rather quickly."

"Oh dear," Ruthanna said, sitting up. "I am sorry to hear that."

Unless Cheryl was reading her wrong, she seemed genuinely surprised to hear that.

"Did you clean Silas's office along with the rest of the house?" Cheryl asked as she took another bite of pie.

Ruthanna nodded. "I did not touch his files or anything inside his desk, but I did straighten the desk and dust the furniture and such."

"Did you ever see anything in there that referenced a deed or that land or anything of that nature?" Cheryl asked.

"No." Ruthanna drank some more coffee and set her mug down. "I do not remember seeing anything like that." She thought for a moment. "There was a file inside the drawer marked Important Papers. Did you see that?"

Cheryl nodded. "It is not in there, sadly." She toyed with her fork for a moment. "Do you have any idea where else he might have kept it?"

"I am sorry," she said. "I really wish I could help you, but I cannot think of any place he might have put the deed. He did not talk to me about his work or business matters."

Cheryl did not doubt this was true. She guessed most Amish men did not share their business affairs with their cleaning girls. But... "Did you ever overhear him say anything about it?"

Ruthanna looked confused for a moment and then laughed. "*Ach.* You are thinking that I might have heard him say something on the telephone. But he did not have a telephone, so no. And he lived alone and didn't have many visitors. I do not know who he could have talked to about this."

Cheryl broke off another small piece of her pie, trying not to shovel it in, and set her fork down gently. There was some sort of spice in the strawberry filling that gave it such an interesting flavor. Sage, maybe?

"Did he have any favorite numbers?" Cheryl asked. "Or any type of code that he liked to use?"

Now the poor Amish girl just looked confused. "I do not know," she said. "He liked numbers, but I do not know if he liked some more than others."

Cheryl believed her and knew it was kind of an odd question. But she refused to believe that the knowledge of how to open that safe had died with Silas.

"If you think of anything that might be helpful, we would very much appreciate it," Naomi said. "This developer, Michael Borland, is trying to buy the land by Friday, and he wants to put a prison on it, so we do not have much time." Cheryl noted that Naomi had already finished her slice of pie, and she didn't feel nearly as bad about how quickly she was downing hers.

"I will," Ruthanna said.

But something in her face had changed. Was she just upset at the idea of the land sale going through so quickly? Or a prison being built in their community? Cheryl wasn't sure, but she thought it was more than that. Her face had drained of color, and her hands, wrapped around the coffee cup, were shaking a little bit.

"I would hate for Levi to lose that land," Ruthanna continued. "Silas would have wanted him to have it." Then, quickly, she glanced over her shoulder at her mother in the next room and then looked back at Cheryl.

"Well, if you think of anything that might help, please let us know," Naomi said as she stood to go.

"I will." Ruthanna stood as well and cast one more glance at her mother, and then she turned back and smiled at her guests again. What was she doing? It was almost as if she were checking to see if her mother was still there. "And please let me know if there is anything I can do to help prepare for the funeral," she said.

Naomi smiled and shook her head. "Just come. That is all Silas would have wanted."

"I will be there." They chattered briefly about the heat wave that was supposed to continue through the next few days as they walked to the door, and then Naomi said something to Ruthanna's mother in Pennsylvania Dutch as they passed the kitchen. They chatted for a few moments, and from the little bit of their language Cheryl understood, she picked up the fact that they were talking about the funeral the next day. Then Naomi said good-bye, and they stepped out.

As they climbed back into the car, Naomi looked at her triumphantly. "That pie was from Bluebell Pie Shop."

"What?" Cheryl had heard of the pie shop, a quaint shop over in Charm operated by two sisters, but she did not immediately recognize it as from there. "How do you know?"

"It was so yummy, and the flavor is unique." She buckled her seat belt. "Besides, Ruthanna is not much of a baker."

Cheryl had to smile. She could totally understand having store-bought pies on hand, especially when it was as good as that. But to Naomi, this was obviously some sort of sign that proved Ruthanna was wealthy. Cheryl didn't really understand it but found it amusing.

"Did you notice how she balked at the end of the conversation?" Cheryl asked, pulling out into the road.

"What do you mean?" Naomi said.

"I don't know. It was weird. It was like she knew something but didn't want to say it," Cheryl said.

Naomi shook her head. "I did not see that."

How had she missed it? Had Cheryl just imagined it? Was she getting so desperate for answers that she was placing guilt where none existed?

Cheryl decided not to pursue it. Instead, she thought about the other Amish person Cheryl wanted to talk to.

"Seth mentioned that Silas had bought the land from an Englisher, and I would love to track him down. But he didn't know the man's name and thought the man Henry King might know."

"Ach. Yes. He mentioned this to me last night. And as we talked about it, I remembered something. There was some sort of dispute about the border of the land, I believe."

"What do you mean?"

Naomi shrugged. "I am sorry, I do not remember the details. All I know is that I have this sense there was some sort of disagreement about the border of the land, and it had to do with the man who owned it before Silas."

"Goodness." This could be important. She had to find out how to get in touch with that English man.

Naomi laughed. "I know what you are thinking." She glanced at the dashboard and then back at Cheryl. "We could go talk to Henry now if you have time. I should make sure he and his wife know about the visitation this afternoon and funeral anyway. You should turn left up here."

"Will do." Cheryl put on her blinker and slowed, but her heartbeat sped up. If there had been a dispute about the land, maybe there was a reason there were no records about it. Was there any chance that could be what was going on? Cheryl wasn't sure but she felt hopeful. Maybe now they would finally get some answers.

CHAPTER SIX

A few minutes later, Cheryl and Naomi were being ushered inside the Kings' home. Henry and his wife Rose lived in a *dawdy haus* behind the main house on a farm bordering the land Levi was to inherit. The house was small but neat and well kept, and it smelled like freshly baked bread. Cheryl's stomach rumbled.

Rose was a short, round woman with gray hair scraped back into a tight bun under her kapp. Her face was warm and her eyes gentle. The two Amish women talked for a moment in Pennsylvania Dutch, and again Cheryl was pretty sure they were discussing the funeral. While they chatted, she looked around the kitchen and took in the cabinets painted a cheerful shade of blue and the plates stacked neatly on the sideboard. Then Rose gestured for them to sit at the table and offered them some freshly baked bread.

"That smells delicious," Naomi said, and Cheryl nodded. Naomi quickly explained why they were there, and after Rose set plates with thick slices of homemade bread topped by creamy homemade butter on the table in front of them, she stepped into the other room and said something to her husband. A moment later, he followed her into the kitchen, nodded at Naomi and Cheryl individually, and then sat down at the head of the table.

Rose slid another thick piece of bread onto the table in front of her husband and sat down at the far end.

"So. Rose tells me you want to know about that property I sold to the Englischer. The one Silas bought."

Cheryl often found Amish men intimidating, with their severe beards and typically stoic nature, and Henry fit the mold, but there was a gentleness in his voice that she found reassuring.

"If you don't mind, we'd certainly appreciate it," Cheryl said.

He nodded, but didn't say anything for a minute, and then he picked up his bread, took a bite, and chewed. Finally, just as Cheryl was beginning to wonder if he would ever answer, he responded.

"I sold that piece of land more than ten years ago. It was the same year Jesse was married, and we needed to build another room on to the house so they would have a place to stay. So I sold the piece of land to pay for it."

Cheryl nodded to show she was following. She broke off a piece of the bread on her plate, and tiny wisps of steam rose up, carrying the yeasty scent upward. It smelled heavenly.

"I sold it to an Englischer named Bryan Rumble, from Cincinnati. He was young, and he and his wife were going to become farmers. Tired of the city life, I guess." He shrugged.

"They did not know much about farming," Rose said.

Cheryl almost laughed at the blunt way she said it. She did not have to share what she really thought for her impression to come through.

"They lived there on the land?" Cheryl hadn't been aware there was a house on the property.

"In a tiny house they built themselves," Henry said. "They had no electricity, no plumbing, and no insulation, as far as I could see." He laughed. "Not much sense either."

"They called it 'living off the grid,'" Rose said.

"It sounds to me like they wanted to be Amish without becoming Amish," Naomi said.

"Oh no. There was nothing Amish about that house. Holes between the planks in the walls big enough to put a shovel through. Sloppy and haphazard." He shook his head. "Best thing was to just tear it down when they left."

"They were nice enough," Rose continued, "but they were always running over here with questions. 'How much should a goat eat? How can I keep rodents from eating my squash plants? Why is this chicken not laying eggs?'"

Her husband laughed at the memory.

"Were you able to help them?" Naomi asked.

"Oh yes. I pointed out that their chicken was a rooster," Rose said, and both Naomi and Henry laughed. Cheryl chuckled, but she wasn't altogether sure she'd be able to tell the difference herself.

"But then they started planting their garden over the property line," Henry said. "At first it was just a row of beans here, a line of spinach. But as the summer went on, the garden expanded, and soon they built a fence around their garden a good twenty-five feet on to our property."

"Did you say anything to them?" Naomi asked.

"Oh yes, several times," Rose said. "At first it seemed like they did not mean to do it, and I believed it. There were so many things they did not understand, and I figured this was one of them. They promised to move their plantings. But then it just continued. We became frustrated."

"What did you do? Once they'd built the fence around the garden, it was clear they weren't going to give up, wasn't it?"

"We were not sure what to do," Henry said. "We did not want to cause problems, but we also did not want them to keep taking more, more, more. We tried and tried to talk with them, but to no avail. Eventually, we decided to consult a lawyer."

"Wait, I thought Amish people didn't sue." Cheryl felt like a dolt, but this was what she'd been led to believe.

"We do everything we can to avoid it," Naomi explained. "But to defend ourselves, sometimes we will."

"But around that time, the city boy and his wife decided farming was too hard, and they moved back to the city."

"And he sold the land to Silas?" Cheryl asked.

"Yes." Henry took another bite. "But they did not take out the garden that was on my land, and Silas and Betty did not realize the garden was not technically theirs to use. So when she started growing vegetables in the garden, we decided not to ask them to move it."

"They were good, God-fearing people," Rose added. "It was not their fault. They did not even know that it wasn't their land. It did not seem fair to ask them to start the garden over for a few square feet of land."

Cheryl tried to imagine any English person she knew simply ceding the land they owned to another person, and she couldn't do it. She admired the Amish more every day. She may not always understand them, but she appreciated them.

"So a part of the land Silas bought wasn't really his to own," Naomi concluded.

"No," Rose said. "But he did not know that."

Cheryl thought for a minute. "Had you actually spoken with a lawyer before you learned that the Englisher, this guy Bryan, was moving?"

Henry nodded. "*Ja*. And he had dug up the plat map." He ripped off a chunk of the bread in front of him. "Why?"

"I am trying to figure out if the disputed border could have caused any problems with the deed," Cheryl said.

Rose tilted her head and scrunched up her face. "Do you think it could have?"

"I don't know," Cheryl admitted. "But I will try to find out. Can you tell me the name of the lawyer you talked to?"

"Oh yes." A look of frustration passed over Rose's face. "His name was Luke Bradshaw."

Cheryl tried to keep her face neutral. "I've heard that he doesn't have the best reputation."

Rose and Henry looked at each other, and then Henry spoke.

"He does not always deal fairly with our people," he said simply. The look on his face showed that he did not intend to say more.

"At the time, he was the only one around here who worked with our people," Rose added.

Well, Cheryl had an appointment to see him later today. She would ask him about this disputed land as well as find out whether he had handled the sale between Silas and this Bryan Rumble.

A clock on the wall dinged, and Cheryl realized it was one o'clock already. Henry heard the noise too and pushed himself up. "I must go help Alvin in the barn now," he said.

"Thank you for your help," Cheryl said.

"We really appreciate it," Naomi added.

"It is no problem. I hope you will get the proof you need so Levi can have his land," Rose said. "And we will see you tomorrow."

Naomi nodded and led Cheryl out. Naomi asked to be dropped off back at her house to prepare for the visitation, and as Cheryl drove her there, she asked more about Silas.

"My husband's brother was a good man," Naomi said. "He was kind to his wife, and they loved each other, though I know it was hard when the *boppli* did not come. Sometimes that can drive a couple apart, but it seemed to bring them closer together."

"It must have been hard for him when she passed away."

"Oh yes." Naomi nodded. "It was very sad. She had been sick for many years, but it was still a shock when she passed. But he carried on. His business helped him stay busy."

Cornfields passed by the car windows in a blur.

"Levi and Seth told me that Betty had gotten forgetful."

"Oh yes. That is one way of putting it," Naomi said.

"And that she sometimes hid things in unusual places."

"I would not say she hid things, necessarily," Naomi said. "She did not mean to hide them, you see. But she would leave things in odd places and forget about them."

"My grandfather got like that toward the end. It was difficult for my grandmother," Cheryl said. "So I understand this is difficult. But...do you know if she had any favorite spots to put things?"

"Ach. You are thinking she may have gotten ahold of the deed and hidden it away somewhere?"

"It's one possibility," Cheryl admitted.

"I do not know where her favorite spots were," Naomi said. "I am afraid that only Silas might have known that, and we cannot ask him."

Cheryl nodded and didn't say anything for a moment. Her car radio was tuned to some news program, and she turned it off and absorbed the quiet. Finally, she ventured, "Is there...do you think there's any chance he could have been mistaken about owning that land?"

"I do not know," Naomi said. "I guess it is possible, but I don't see how. It is not the kind of thing one gets wrong."

"Unless there was some sort of dispute about the border," Cheryl said. "That might have caused problems."

"Maybe." Naomi didn't look convinced.

Cheryl tried to figure out how to word this next question. "You said Seth's family arrives later today, right?"

"Yes," Naomi said. "His brother Emmon and his family, as well as Emmon's wife's sister and her family, will be coming this afternoon, just in time for the viewing."

"Did Silas have any other family?" Cheryl asked.

"One sister, Barbara, but she lives in Delaware and will not make it for the funeral. His parents live with her, but his father is in very bad health, and he cannot travel. His mother is devastated to miss it, but she must stay with her husband. And there were two other brothers, but they are passed. Aside from Betty's family, that is all."

"And Emmon is set to inherit the house and main parcel of land, right?"

"Yes."

"Could we ask if they know anything about it when they arrive?"

"Of course."

Cheryl briefly wondered if Emmon could have had anything to do with the deed going missing but decided there was no good way to ask about that. Besides, he had nothing to gain from the land passing out of the family and a lot to lose if a jail was built next to the land. Even if he didn't intend to live in the house in Sugarcreek, it would no doubt lose some of its value being next to such a facility. Still, she was hopeful that Silas's brother Emmon would know something that they'd missed.

"It sounds like you will have quite a full house."

"Oh yes," Naomi said. "Funerals always do bring lots of people together." She turned in her seat and looked at Cheryl. "Have you ever been to an Amish funeral?"

"No." She didn't even know what they were like. She imagined they must be pretty different from English funerals but couldn't imagine how so.

"Would you like to come?"

"Are you serious?"

"Cheryl, I would not joke about a funeral," Naomi said. Cheryl laughed. No, her friend probably wouldn't joke about that.

"I wouldn't be intruding?"

"Not at all. You would be very welcome."

Cheryl had to admit she was intrigued. And she would be able to show support for her friends at this difficult time. Plus, she couldn't help but think it might be a good time to observe Seth's family and see if there was anyone who was behaving strangely. Though, honestly, she wasn't sure she would be able to identify what strange Amish behavior looked like, since most of what they did seemed strange to her.

"I would be honored."

"You are welcome at the visitation this afternoon as well. It starts at four o'clock."

That was when Cheryl's appointment with Luke Bradshaw was. With the closing coming up so soon, she didn't want to risk missing her chance to talk with him.

"I don't think I'll be able to make that, but I will gladly come to the funeral."

"Good. It is at nine a.m. at our house."

Cheryl realized that if she went to the funeral, she would need to close the shop or find someone to work at the shop in her place, since both Esther and Lydia had asked for the day off to attend the funeral. Well, she'd worry about that later.

When they arrived at Naomi's house, she dropped her friend off, and she instinctively looked around, searching for Levi.

"He is over at the cemetery digging the grave," Naomi said, smiling gently.

Cheryl felt her cheeks redden.

"But he will meet you at Silas's house at two, when the locksmith comes," she said.

Cheryl nodded, and Naomi winked and stepped out of the car. Cheryl still had a little time before she needed to head back to Silas's house. She would swing by the Swiss Miss and see how things were going.

"I'm back," she called as she stepped inside. She breathed in deeply. The sight of the little shop never failed to bring her joy. Lydia was dusting the display of wooden toys, while Esther was running a broom around the floor in the nook at the front of the shop. Both girls looked up and nodded, acknowledging the obvious.

"Did you have a nice time?" Lydia asked.

"It was productive," Cheryl said.

"Where did you go?" Esther asked.

"Your mother and I just stopped by Henry and Rose King's house, and before that we went to see Ruthanna Yutzy," she said, settling in behind the counter. The shop was in one of those strange lulls where no customers came in, and Cheryl was grateful for a few moments of peace. She logged on to her e-mail and saw that Pam from the library had sent her a message with a of couple attachments.

"Ruthanna Yutzy?" Lydia called out to Esther. "Isn't she the one who used to go out with that Englischer with the fancy car?"

"I think so," Esther said. "She was Ruthanna Zook then, so I do not think they are seeing each other anymore."

"She dated an Englisher?"

"Yes. Some business guy or something. What was his name?"

Esther shrugged. "I do not know. I just remember that all the guys in our district were upset."

Lydia laughed. "Ja, they were, weren't they?" She ran the feather duster over the small shelf. "Borland. I think his last name was Borland. It sounded like Boring to me."

"Borland?" That name caught Cheryl's attention. It seemed like an awfully strange coincidence. Men like Michael Borland didn't usually date Amish girls…but then, Ruthanna was an extraordinarily attractive girl. *Could* she have dated him?

If it was true…Cheryl's mind swirled with the implications. It would explain how Michael knew about the piece of land in the first place. Ruthanna would have had a very good reason to destroy or "lose" Silas's copy of the deed, so her then-boyfriend could purchase it for a song. And Ruthanna *had* acted strangely when Cheryl mentioned Michael's name earlier. Naomi hadn't seen it, but Cheryl knew she hadn't been imagining it. Ruthanna had been hiding something after all. Cheryl wanted to know what else she was hiding.

The Amish girls returned to their work, chattering away in Pennsylvania Dutch and Cheryl turned back to the e-mail from Pam. She clicked on it and was pleased to see that Pam had found the full-text articles about Michael Borland from the Canton *Repository* and had attached them to the e-mail as pdfs. Cheryl clicked on them eagerly.

Local Amish Upset about Shopping Center

Charm, Ohio. Many residents of Holmes County are looking forward to the new Country Corner shopping center set to open off Route 557 in December. The shopping center, which was approved by the zoning board in controversial closed-door meetings last spring, is being built by Borland Developers, a local firm that has recently been taken over by the owner's ambitious eldest son.

"I am so excited that we are finally getting a Starbucks around here," said local resident Mikayla Grover, who works at a nearby doctor's office and grew up in the area. "I will go there, like, every day."

But not everyone is so thrilled about the prospect.

Zeke Hershberger, a local Amish man, has filed a lawsuit alleging that the land for the center was taken from his family illegally. He declined to be interviewed for this story, but according to public records, his lawyer Luke Bradshaw filed a suit to try to block the construction of the center after learning that a parcel of land that had belonged to his deceased father had been reclaimed by the county after the family failed to pay taxes on the land. Hershberger alleges that the family never received any bills from the county.

This is not the first project Borland Developers has been involved with that has run into legal trouble and accusations of unfair treatment of the Amish. The Poplar

Village apartments that the firm built last year were also plagued by suspicion and accusations that the land had been taken from Amish neighbors unfairly.

Cheryl read through the article again, taking in as much information as she could. She then clicked on the next document Pam had sent. It was a follow-up article about the sizeable legal settlement Borland Developers had paid to sort out the mess. There was one more article about a different plot of land, which had been used to build the Poplar Village apartments referenced in the previous article. It had also been obtained through less-than-standard means, also from an Amish family.

Huh. Cheryl leaned back and stretched her legs out in front of her. Well, this certainly cast Michael Borland in a bad light. That, plus the fact of his connection to the Amish cleaning girl, who could easily have found and removed Silas's copy of the deed without his knowledge, pointed to a likely explanation of what had happened in this case.

Cheryl needed to talk to Michael Borland. He hadn't called since her visit yesterday, so she pulled up the picture of the business card and tried again, leaving a message with his annoyed receptionist.

Cheryl also needed to talk with Ruthanna Yutzy again. She'd have to find a way to get her to tell her the truth this time.

She checked the clock. There was still a bit of time before she had to leave.

Well, first things first. If she was going to go to the funeral tomorrow, she needed to figure out what to do with the store. She hated to simply not open, but if she couldn't get someone to come in and work during the funeral, that was what she would have to do. Fortunately, Cheryl had an idea.

Kinsley Coleman was a teenager Cheryl had hired to help out when she had been in town to visit her grandparents during the Christmas season. Cheryl had run into Kinsley's grandmother just last week, and she had been excited that Kinsley would be spending a few weeks with her after school got out. Cheryl called Kinsley now, and Kinsley was excited about the idea of picking up some hours at the Swiss Miss while she was in town. She had spent enough time in the shop over Christmas that Cheryl felt confident she could handle things, and Cheryl talked with her about where she would leave the key so Kinsley could open up and what to do when she got here. She got off the phone feeling confident that the store would be in good hands while she and Lydia and Esther all attended Silas's funeral.

There was still a bit of time before she had to go to Silas's house to meet the locksmith. She briefly considered popping over to the Honey Bee for a sandwich, but she thought about how long the line had been this morning and decided she didn't have that much time. Molly Bakker, of the Village Inn Bed-and-Breakfast, was supposed to be running the café at this point, according to the schedule, and while Cheryl wouldn't mind seeing her, she decided to focus instead on using this time to help unravel the mystery. Besides, after the pie and the homemade bread, she wasn't very hungry.

While her first instinct was to immediately get back into her car and go to Ruthanna's house and demand she tell her the truth, she decided that was unlikely to produce the result she was hoping for. Ruthanna hadn't been truthful before, so why would she suddenly open up to Cheryl now? She needed to think about how to get Ruthanna to tell her what she really knew. In the meantime, she would take advantage of the lull and see what she could learn about this Bryan Rumble, the Englisher who had slowly conscripted more and more of Henry King's land. It had been a long time ago, but he might have a copy of the sales documents in his files. Maybe there was something in them that could prove the land belonged to Silas.

Henry King had said that Bryan was from Cincinnati. Cheryl didn't have a Cincinnati phone book here, and though the library might have one, she felt like she'd called in enough favors for the day there. There was no way to know whether he still lived in Cincinnati anyway. She decided the most likely way to find contact information for him would be to look online. She glanced around the shop. An older couple wearing T-shirts from Cedar Point amusement park came in, but otherwise the store was quiet.

She turned back to her laptop computer on the counter and pulled up a browser window. She typed in the name *Bryan Rumble*.

The first link that came up was an obituary in a Cincinnati newspaper. Cheryl clicked on the link and read the piece. Bryan Rumble had died in a car accident over Labor Day weekend a few years back, she read. He'd owned a landscaping business in the suburbs of Cincinnati, and he was survived by his wife Allison and daughter Liza.

Well. Cheryl sat back in her chair. This was not good news. She would not be getting any information from Bryan about that property sale. Could his wife Allison have any of the old records from their time as farmers? Cheryl didn't know, but it was worth checking. She searched for the name Allison Rumble and was directed to the Web site for a high school in the same town where Bryan had lived. Scrolling through the site, she discovered that Allison Rumble was a history teacher there. Her e-mail address was posted online.

Cheryl tried to figure out how to word her e-mail. Finally, she decided to simply explain that she lived in Sugarcreek and was interested in the property that they had owned when they lived there. She hit Send and hoped her message would be intriguing enough that Allison would reply.

"Cheryl? Is it not time for you to go to Uncle Silas's house?"

Cheryl looked up at the cuckoo clock on the wall and saw that Esther was right. She needed to get going if she was going to meet the locksmith to get that safe open. Esther and Lydia assured her that they could handle the shop, and a few minutes later she was pulling up in front of Silas's house. A buggy was already there, and the horse Sugar was unhitched and enjoying a drink of water from a trough by the barn.

She knocked on the door, and Levi invited her to step inside. He and Seth were in the office.

"We were thinking Daed could continue looking in the workshop," Levi said. "And I would keep looking through the files in the office while the locksmith was here. You could look through the rest of the house for more of Aunt Betty's hiding places."

"I think that makes sense," Cheryl said. Seth nodded and walked out to the workshop, and just as she was about to head to the office, a car pulled into the driveway. The logo for a key shop was pasted on the side door.

"I'll bring him in," Cheryl said, and Levi nodded. She went to the door and found a man with graying brown hair and a mustache. Smiley's Key Shop was embroidered on the pocket of his shirt. An anthropomorphic safe, with hands and feet and eyeballs, was under the words.

"You called for a locksmith?" he said, and Cheryl recognized the nasal voice from the phone. "I'm Alan." He shifted the small bag he carried to his left hand and held out his right to shake hers.

"I'm Cheryl. Thank you so much for coming. Please, come in." He stepped in and looked around the plain room with the simple furniture and, beyond Cheryl, the icebox and kerosene stove. Then he looked back at Cheryl with confusion apparent on his face.

"This is not my house," she explained. "It belonged to an Amish man, and he passed away. We're trying to get into the safe in his office."

"Ah." He nodded. "All right then. Show me the way."

"It's just in here." Cheryl led him down the hall and into the office and showed him the safe and introduced Levi. Alan took in the simple wooden furniture and the cross-stitched Bible verse hung on the wall and nodded.

"Thank you for coming to help us," Levi said. He was looking through a file folder in the middle of the second drawer of files. It would take him weeks to get through all the files at this rate.

"Nothing I love more than busting open one of these things," the man said, eyeing the safe. "And this one's a beaut. One hundred numbers on that dial. This is gonna be fun." He seemed perversely excited by the prospect.

"We would like to avoid damaging the door if possible," Cheryl said.

"Oh yeah. I won't try to pry it off or anything. I'm going to try to crack the code here."

"How will you do that?" Levi had stopped going through the files and was watching as the locksmith knelt down in front of the safe and spun the dial.

"Most safes make a small noise or give a little resistance when you get to the right numbers," Alan explained. He reached into his small bag and pulled out what looked like a kind of stethoscope and then put the ends up to his ears. "I'm going to start by listening."

"Will it bother you if we're going through these files?" she asked, indicating the filing cabinets. Cheryl knew she was supposed to be searching through the rest of the house, but she was so curious to see how he did this.

"It shouldn't, but I will let you know."

He pressed the end of his tool against the safe and started slowly turning the dial. Cheryl moved to the far end of the filing cabinets, which she soon discovered was for couch and sofa files, and started from the bottom, carefully going through each folder, looking for—exactly what, she didn't know.

From what she could tell, each folder contained the name and address of the piece's owner, the date the piece was brought in, a

sketch of the piece, which was initialed by both the owner and
Silas, and a handwritten sales receipt. Cheryl eyed the drawers
upon drawers of these. What exactly did they think they were
going to find in here? Surely there must be places to look for the
deed that would be less, well, hopeless?

"Sixty-two."

"What?" Cheryl looked up to see the locksmith grinning at her.

"The first number in the combination is sixty-two."

"Really?" That hadn't taken him long. Her spirits began to rise.
They would have that thing open in no time. "Fantastic."

Levi nodded, showing his approval.

"Well, the next two numbers will probably take longer to
come across," he said.

Still, she turned back to the filing cabinets with renewed vigor.

But thirty minutes later, there was still no progress. Cheryl had
made it halfway through one drawer of files, and Levi wasn't
moving any faster. This was hopeless. And to make matters worse,
the locksmith got an emergency call—a woman had been locked
out of her house with her baby inside and the stove on. Even
Cheryl couldn't argue that cracking Silas's safe was more important
than getting that woman's door open. Alan promised to return the
next afternoon and rushed out of the house.

She was starting to push herself up to go search the kitchen for
hiding places when Seth came in come from the workshop holding
a small metal box.

"I think I found something."

CHAPTER SEVEN

Cheryl and Levi both hurried over to Seth to see what he had found in the workshop. He stepped forward and set the metal box down on the table. It was about the size of the box her checks used to come in, but it was made of some sort of metal that had started rusting a bit along one edge. There was a handle on top, hinges along one side, and clasps on the front.

"I found this at the back of a drawer in an old workbench at the far end of the workshop. I do not believe he used the workbench anymore because there were many odds and ends piled on top of it. But look."

Seth flipped up the clasps and used the handle to lift the lid, and they all leaned forward to see what was inside.

Seth reached in and lifted out a small cream-colored envelope with the number 415 written on it. It was roughly the size of an index card. He flipped the flap open and tipped the envelope over, and out slid a small key.

"What in the world?" Cheryl picked up the key and held it up. "Is this for the safe?"

"There is no keyhole on the safe," Levi said, eyeing it.

"I wonder what it could be for?" Cheryl said, turning the key over in her hands. It was about the same size as a typical house key, but the metal was thinner, with a round head, and the teeth were square.

"It does not look like a house key," Levi said. Cheryl nodded. And obviously it wasn't a car key—the shape of it was wrong, and what would Silas be doing with a car key? The truth was, chances were it didn't open anything important. Seth had found it buried at the back of a drawer in an unused section of the workshop. It wasn't exactly where you kept something important. It probably went to a lock that was long gone.

"Maybe a padlock? Are there any out in the workshop?" Levi asked.

But what about that envelope? And the number 415? Those kept it from being an automatic throwaway. The key had been carefully labeled and hidden away. If they could figure out what 415 meant, maybe that would lead them to the right place.

"I will go look," Seth said and handed Cheryl the envelope and went back out to the workshop. Levi returned to the file drawer, and Cheryl turned the key over in her hands again, trying to figure out what it could be for.

It looked vaguely familiar. But where had she seen a key like this before? It pulled at the edges of her mind. Finally, Cheryl gave up trying to remember, and she pulled out her phone and pulled up a search window. She typed in the number 415 into the browser to see what came up.

Hmm. 415 was the area code for San Francisco and a good chunk of the Bay Area. Cheryl didn't know of any Amish connection to that region and doubted that meant anything. There were various State Road 415s, but none in Ohio. She searched through pages of results, but none of them looked useful. But just as she was about to put her phone away and keep searching through the drawers, she noticed the time.

"Goodness. I need to get going," she said. "I have an appointment to talk to the lawyer, Luke Bradshaw, soon."

Levi said he and Seth needed to leave shortly anyway to get home for the viewing. She tried not to let her frustration show. They hadn't gotten any closer to finding Silas's copy of the deed today.

She threw the car into gear, turned around, and pulled out on to the country road. Now that Levi and Naomi had pointed it out, the car did make a pretty loud screech when she accelerated. Huh. She'd have to try to find time to take the car in soon. But not right now. Now she had an appointment to keep.

A few minutes later, she pulled up in front of a stately Victorian house at the edge of town. It was painted white and surrounded by a lush green lawn, and a sign that said Bradshaw, Dobson, and Holtzclaw was planted in front.

A receptionist looked up as Cheryl entered, a woman who looked to be about her mother's age, with graying hair and a round face. She smiled as Cheryl entered. She was in what would have been the parlor of the house originally, and it still had decorative molding around the edge of the ceiling and a brick fireplace against one wall. The chairs and small side table in the waiting area looked to be antiques. Once again, Cheryl hoped she wasn't being charged by the minute to be here. This place didn't look cheap.

"Hello. I'm here to see Luke Bradshaw," she said.

The woman nodded, picked up the phone, and called the lawyer. Cheryl noticed that the elastic gather on the sleeve of her shirt was too tight and had left a mark.

"You can go right on back," the receptionist said, her voice deep but pleasant. "Second door on the left."

Cheryl thanked her and went through a wooden door to the right of the reception desk. The walls were covered with floral wallpaper, and the polished wooden floorboards creaked beneath her feet as she headed toward the second door on the left.

When she got there, the door was open, and she knocked on it gently. A trim, balding man in a dark suit looked up. Cheryl guessed he was in his late fifties, and he looked up from his computer screen and gestured for Cheryl to come inside.

"You must be Cheryl Cooper," the man said, rising. He held out his hand, and Cheryl shook it and then sat down in the high-backed chair he indicated. His desk was a carved mahogany, polished to a high sheen, and the shelves behind his desk were lined with rows and rows of thick, leather-covered volumes. There was a beautiful, rich wool Oriental rug on the floor. Cheryl couldn't believe the contrast between this opulent place and the simple Amish farmhouse she'd just left.

"I am. Thank you for seeing me."

"Not a problem." He wore glasses with big round lenses that made him look a little bit surprised, and something about the way they didn't quite fit with his sharp suit was endearing. "Sherry tells me your question is not legal in nature."

He spoke with just the slightest hint of a Southern drawl.

"No, it's not." His diploma from Mississippi State and his law degree from Ohio State hung in a heavy wooden frame. It was impressive, intimidating. But on his desk was a photo of himself with a woman and three teenagers, presumably his wife and kids, in front of a Broadway theater, which she found charming, and there was a kindness in his voice that made her feel at ease. "I'm here with something of a strange question. I'm friendly with an Amish family, the Millers, and I'm trying to find some information about a Silas Miller. I believe you drew up his will."

"Let's see." Luke smiled. "That's right. Silas Miller. Long beard, hat, suspenders?" He winked. That basically described every Amish man around here. "I'm just kidding. I do remember him. I drew it up initially maybe five years ago or so?"

Cheryl wasn't actually sure when it had been, but she nodded.

"And then he contacted me a few months back about it again. That must have been November or so."

"He did?" This was news. The lawyer nodded.

"Is there a problem with the will?"

"Not exactly," Cheryl said. "You see, Silas Miller passed away a few days back."

"I'm very sorry to hear that." He sounded genuine. Either this man was a very good liar or the tales she'd heard about how awful he was had been exaggerated. "Did the family find the will? If not, I can provide a copy."

"No, that's okay. They have that. The problem is, the title for a piece of land he willed to his nephew Levi seems to have gone missing. I'm trying to help them find it before the land gets sold off by the county."

"Oh dear." He leaned back in his chair.

"I was told you were one of the few lawyers in these parts who worked with the Amish ten years ago, when he bought the land, and I was hoping you might have handled the sale and have some record of it."

"Ah. I see." He rested his hands on his belly and threaded his fingers together. "Yes, it's likely I did handle the sale. You're right that for many years I was one of the few lawyers around here who worked with the Amish. I would need to go back through my files and see if I still have any record of the sale. I usually try to keep a copy of everything, just in case, but it's been so long that I don't know if I've still got it."

Cheryl's heart lightened. This was it. Here was the solution. She just needed to have him find the paperwork for the sale and she would be set.

"That's wonderful. Do you think there's any chance you could have it before Friday? That's when the county is trying to close on the sale of the land."

"That quickly?" He sat up straighter in his chair. "Didn't you say he just passed away recently?"

"That's right. The developer who is trying to buy the land is pushing it through quickly."

"Oh dear." He shook his head. "I think I might have a guess as to who the developer is."

"He seems to have something of a reputation for this sort of thing."

"So it is Borland Developers?"

Cheryl nodded.

"This type of situation has come up before with them," the lawyer said. "They are quite good at getting the proper process thrown right out the window to get the land they want quickly."

Cheryl nodded. "I read that you represented another Amish farmer who was in this situation. He hadn't gotten his tax bills and the county took his land?"

"Yes, that was a sad case." He paused. "Though, in that case, the man really hadn't paid his taxes. He had been sent bills and warnings for many months, and he'd been ignoring them, unfortunately. The county wasn't really wrong to take the land. What was wrong was how they went about it and how quickly the land was sold off, before we had a chance to fight it."

"I thought you said he'd been getting the bills for months?"

"He had. But he didn't contact me until after the sale was announced, and by then it was too late. Borland Developers did whatever they do to get things moving, and the sale proceeded too quickly."

"I'd really love to get this sale stopped before it's too late. Is there any way to get the paperwork from the sale of the land pulled quickly?"

"I don't know about that. The old files are kept in an off-site storage facility. It usually takes about a week to get the files pulled."

His chair squeaked as he sat up and scooted toward the desk. "The county should have a record of the sale if you need it quicker though."

"That's the problem. They don't. And Silas's deed is missing, which means we need to find a way to prove that land was his right away."

"Oh dear."

"The worst part is, Borland Developers wants to build a jail on the property. Is there any way to expedite the search for the records? I know it's crazy, but I am desperate to find some way to prove the land is not the county's to sell."

"Goodness. A jail?" The man held up one finger, telling her to wait, and then turned to his computer and typed out an e-mail message. "No doubt the entire community would have serious objections to that. That is probably why they are rushing it through." He hit Send, and then he turned back to Cheryl. "I've asked Sherry to get that file pulled right away. Our paralegal is on vacation this week, but we'll do everything we can."

"Thank you. I appreciate it."

"In the meantime, have your Amish friends talked about filing an injunction to block the sale? I know quite a good lawyer."

Cheryl smiled. "That is what I am trying to convince them to do. And they might. But so far, they are hoping to solve this without resorting to legal recourse."

"Ah. Because the Amish don't like to sue."

Cheryl hesitated. He was partly right.

"I see. And because they don't trust me."

Cheryl didn't know what to say, but it seemed her silence was enough to confirm his suspicions.

"I know a lot of the Amish around here have heard rumors about me, about how I cheated someone or didn't play fairly. Is that part of what's going on here?"

Reluctantly, Cheryl nodded.

He sighed. "Unfortunately, I have heard those rumors too, and I've seen my business with the Amish drop precipitously in the past few years. But I assure you, I have not done anything to treat any of my clients, Amish or not, unfairly."

"Then why do they all think you did?"

He reached out and grabbed a pen from the holder on his desk and started turning it over in his hands.

"Misunderstandings," he said simply.

Cheryl tilted her head. Could simple misunderstandings really explain what she'd heard about this man?

"I believe it all started after Gabriel Esch. He wanted me to prosecute his next-door neighbor for playing loud music, but I couldn't. As much as I sympathize with him, his neighbor didn't technically break any laws. Gabriel was fed up and frustrated, and he finally made up his mind to do something about it, and then I had to tell him what he wanted me to do wasn't within the bounds of the law. But he didn't seem to understand that."

Cheryl thought about this. It sounded plausible enough. But could such an innocuous event really be the cause of so much distrust?

"And then, shortly after that, I had started the paperwork for an Amish family to buy a house. But once the appraisal came back, it turned out that the house had been overpriced, and the banks wouldn't lend the family the money to buy the house after all. The deal fell apart, but I still billed them for the hours of work I had put in. Well, the way they saw it, I was trying to take money from them when I hadn't done my job, but that wasn't the case at all."

He paused, thinking, and then he continued. "And then there was the mess with Zeke Hershberger and his tax bills. I couldn't stop the sale, and he thought bringing in a lawyer would fix everything, so he was upset. That one really blew up."

He was quiet for a moment, and then he continued.

"The Amish are good people. Strong, solid, trustworthy people." He took a deep breath. "But…they don't have the strongest educations. Sometimes complicated legal matters…" He struggled to come up with the right words. "Well, in my experience, they don't always understand the nuances of the law."

Cheryl considered this. She knew that Amish typically ended their education at eighth grade. In her experience, the Amish were as bright and insightful as most Englishers she knew and more thoughtful as a rule, but she could see his point. Without advanced education, the nuances of the law would be incomprehensible to most people, and she could see how that, coupled with the inherent differences in lifestyle and worldview, could lead to misunderstandings.

"It doesn't take long for word to travel among the Amish," Luke continued.

Well, Cheryl could agree with that. She had seen the "Amish telephone" at work herself.

"One person thinks he was cheated, and suddenly the whole community thinks I'm a liar."

He tapped his pen against the blotter on his desk.

"This is why many of the lawyers in the region prefer not to engage with the Amish. It can be very difficult to work with them. But I have been around long enough and seen how special and unique these communities are, and I want to help them however I can. I swear to you, I have only tried to do my best for my clients."

Cheryl wanted to believe him. Something in him did feel trustworthy. But she wasn't sure.

"If your friends decide they do need a lawyer to try to block the sale, I would be happy to represent them for free," he said. "To try to show them how serious I am."

"That's very generous," Cheryl said. She had a feeling that would help make it easier for Seth and Naomi to consider filing an injunction, though they would still consider it carefully. "I will let them know."

"They will need to do it quickly, though, if the sale is scheduled for Friday. I'd have to get before the judge tomorrow."

Cheryl nodded. It was Wednesday afternoon, and she knew that they didn't have much time. But she also knew that pressuring the Amish would have the opposite of the desired effect.

"And I will try to get those records pulled as soon as possible," Luke said.

Cheryl thanked him and then stood to go. It wasn't until she'd gotten outside that she realized no one had asked for her billing information.

She climbed into her car, thinking maybe Luke Bradshaw was not so bad after all. It didn't mean he was off her list of suspects, but after talking with him she was leaning toward thinking he wasn't as bad a guy as her Amish friends made him out to be.

Cheryl noticed that she had a voice mail. It must have come in while she was talking with the lawyer. She put her phone to her ear and listened to a message from a Nancy Chandler, who introduced herself as a reporter from the *Times-Reporter.* She said Jessica Stockton had given her the number. Nancy said she wanted to speak with Cheryl about the land Michael Borland was trying to buy from under the Amish farmer and the rumors that he was planning to build a jail on the land. She left her number and asked Cheryl to call her back.

Well, now. This could help get things moving. She eagerly dialed the number Nancy had left.

"Nancy Chandler."

"Hi. This is Cheryl Cooper. You left me a voice mail regarding the..."

"Oh yes, yes. Thank you for calling me back. So tell me about this jail that's going up."

The woman talked really quickly, but Cheryl managed to keep up. She told her the whole story, from finding out that someone had made an offer on the land to the missing deed to the information about the proposed jail. Nancy interrupted several times throughout the process, but Cheryl finally got it all out. Nancy thanked her and promised to start working on a story. She was sure there would be a lot of interest from the community about the jail and about another deal from the developer who had repeatedly cheated the Amish out of their land.

Cheryl hung up, satisfied. Hopefully if the community rose up in protest, the sale would be blocked, whether or not they could find Silas's deed.

She had been planning to head back toward the Swiss Miss, but now she was all riled up. So when she got into the car, she turned the other way, back toward the farm where Ruthanna Yutzy lived. Ruthanna was hiding something, and Cheryl resolved to find out what it was.

She carefully retraced the way she'd driven earlier today, and with only a couple of U-turns, she found her way to the Yutzy farm. A man in Amish dress was opening the door of the barn, and she waved a greeting then carefully climbed the steps and knocked.

"Oh." Ruthanna stepped back when she saw Cheryl on the porch. Her cheeks were flushed, and she was wiping her hands on her apron. "You're back." She stood in the doorway, hesitating. She looked behind her toward the kitchen and then back at Cheryl. "I did not expect you."

No, Cheryl imagined she didn't. Ruthanna was obviously thrown off, which was good.

"I was hoping I could ask you a few more questions," Cheryl said. "About the sale of that land we talked about earlier."

Ruthanna pulled the door a bit more closed, so her body was blocking the only space.

"This is not a very good time. I must get dinner on the table."

"It will just take a second." Cheryl had very rarely been turned away from an Amish home. That just wasn't something the Amish did. Ruthanna didn't want to talk to her. "I just wanted to know why you didn't tell me that you had dated Michael Borland, the same developer who is trying to take the land from Levi."

"I . . ." The girl faltered. "I do not know what you are talking about," she said. But she was lying. Cheryl could see it written plain on her face.

"I am talking about the fact that you dated the developer who is trying to buy the land now that the title for Silas's land has disappeared from the county records. You knew this earlier, and you didn't say anything when I asked about the deed to the land, and now I want to know why. Is it because you had something to do with that deed disappearing from Silas's house? Was it something you and your developer boyfriend worked out together?"

Cheryl knew she was being harsh, but she didn't care. Her redhead temper was coming out. If this girl had conspired with the developer to steal the proof that Silas owned the land, she didn't care if she hurt her feelings. She wanted the truth.

"No. That is not true," Ruthanna said. She had recovered a bit and seemed less flustered than she had a few moments before, but she was still shaking her head, like she was trying to make the words disappear. Cheryl waited for her to say more, but the girl once again looked over her shoulder into the house and then pulled the door closed as much as she could while keeping her body in the gap.

"So why didn't you mention your relationship with Michael earlier, when I said his name?"

Ruthanna hesitated and then shook her head. "I am sorry. I cannot answer these questions now. I must get back to making dinner."

And with that, she stepped back and closed the door, and Cheryl was left standing on the doorstep.

Well. That had certainly never happened to her in an Amish home before. Cheryl stood still for a minute, thinking through what had just happened.

She hadn't found out what she had been hoping to learn—whether Ruthanna had conspired with Michael Borland to destroy the evidence that Silas owned that land—but she was now certain that Ruthanna knew something. Cheryl felt frustration and excitement bubble up together. Excitement because this was the first solid lead she'd gotten in this whole mess. Frustration because she wasn't sure how to get Ruthanna to admit whatever it was she knew.

Still, she couldn't stand here on the porch forever, so she turned and climbed back into her car and headed back toward the Swiss Miss. It was time to close up shop for the day.

"I really owe you for all that you did here today," Cheryl said to Lydia as she balanced the register.

Lydia gave her a strange look. "You are paying me to be here. You do not owe me more than that."

Cheryl laughed. She loved how literal the Amish could sometimes be.

"Well, I'm thankful anyway," she said and waved good-bye as Lydia headed out the door. It only took Cheryl a little while longer to finish closing up the shop, and then she turned out the lights, locked the door, and stepped outside.

The sun was beginning to move lower in the sky, but it was still hot as blazes as she made her way across the street to the Honey Bee. The café usually closed just about this time, and Cheryl was glad to see that the last remaining customers were tossing their plates in the bins by the trash cans and doctoring their coffee drinks. Greta Yoder stood behind the counter, looking down at stacks of money next to the register.

"How did it go?" Cheryl asked.

Greta looked up and grimaced. "I hope I did not lose Kathy too many customers today." Short and stout, Greta had a round face and a warm smile.

"I'm sure you did a great job." Greta, along with her husband August, ran Yoder's Corner, a family-style restaurant just down the street. If anyone could handle running a busy café, it was Greta.

Cheryl nodded at the piles of money. "What is all this?"

Greta grinned sheepishly. "I could not figure out how to use this fancy cash register. It is not like the one we have at our restaurant."

Cheryl laughed. She hadn't thought about that. At Yoder's Corner they used an old-fashioned register, with actual metal levers you had to push to open the drawer, just like Cheryl did at her shop. But at the Honey Bee, they used a modern touch-screen tablet system, where customers could run a credit card through a small plastic square and then sign for their food and add the tip electronically right there on the screen. Touch-screen tablets were so ubiquitous and so intuitive that Cheryl hadn't even thought about the fact that the Amish business owners helping Kathy out might not know how to use one.

"Several people tried to use credit cards, but I told them they could not. They did not have cash so I ended up giving their food away for free," Greta said, shaking her head. "I will pay Kathy back for those myself. The rest of the money is here." She patted the piles.

"I'm sure Kathy won't ask you to pay her back for those sandwiches," Cheryl said. She moved around behind the counter and opened the register and started emptying it. Kathy had shown her the small safe in the back where she kept cash overnight, and after she counted and recorded the day's sales, she would stow it all in there. If only she could get Silas's safe open as easily.

"And I could not figure out that fancy kaffee machine." Greta gestured to the espresso machine. "I tried, but after a few very bad lattes, I gave up and only served drip kaffee."

Cheryl nodded. Even the drip coffee machine was more complicated than the percolator she knew the Amish typically used at home. She should have thought about that ahead of time.

"Other than problems with the register and the espresso machine, how did it go?" Cheryl continued.

"It was very busy," Greta said. "We have many sandwiches leftover, but we are clean out of desserts." She indicated the pastry case, which sat mostly empty. "A large group of Amish who journeyed for Silas Miller's funeral came and bought them all."

"Ah. So I guess they made it."

"And I guess they were hungry," Greta said.

Cheryl had to laugh. She knew the Amish had just as good a sense of humor as anyone else, but it still surprised her sometimes.

"They had had a long drive. I expect they were ready for something to eat."

"Drive?"

Greta nodded. "They chartered two vans. You did not expect them to come all the way from Michigan by buggy, did you?"

Now that she thought about it, that was pretty silly.

Greta grabbed a clean rag and started to wipe down the counters.

"You don't have to do that," Cheryl said, gesturing to the rag. "You have a family to get back to. I can clean things up."

"I feel as though I should help so at least I have done something useful here today. I do not know how to use this register or coffee machine, but I do know how to clean."

"Well, thank you," Cheryl said. She started counting the cash.

"It was nice that so many of Silas's relatives were able to come for the funeral," Greta said, rinsing out the rag and wringing it in the sink. "The young ones were so cute."

"Yes, it will be such a comfort to the family to have them there." Then she thought about what Greta had said. "How many children were there in the group?"

"I do not know. Perhaps half a dozen."

"Huh." But then, she guessed they couldn't just leave the children at home while they traveled. "What will they do with the kids during the funeral? Will there be babysitting?"

Greta gave her a strange look. "Babysitting at the funeral?"

"So the kids don't have to see the body and all that?"

Again, Greta seemed confused by the question. "The *kinder* will attend the funeral."

"Oh." Cheryl thought about the funerals at her parents' church. They usually opened the nursery and had someone watch the kids, both so the parents didn't have to worry about whether the children would behave and also because most parents weren't sure funerals were good for young children. Cheryl wasn't sure herself. Could kids really handle seeing a body or understand what death really meant? And the raw grief so often on display—wasn't it better to shield them from that? "They don't get freaked out?"

"Freaked out?" Greta shook her head. "No, they do not."

Cheryl realized she needed to explain before Greta decided she was nuts.

"Often, at English funerals, children are kept away, to protect them from all the talk about death and such."

Greta tilted her head. "Why would you do this? Do not kinder need to understand death just as much as everyone else?"

"I . . ." Cheryl tried to figure out how to answer that. "A lot of people believe it's hard for kids to understand what death really means, and it's better to shield them from that reality while they're still young."

"Ach." Greta turned on the faucet and rinsed out her rag. "I see. We do not agree. Death is a part of life, and the sooner kinder understand that, the sooner they will begin to give thanks to Gott for every day of life."

Cheryl thought about this. It did seem to make some sense, letting children understand from a young age that they were not invincible, that God numbered their days.

"I guess I never thought about it like that," Cheryl said.

Greta nodded, water running over her fingers. "It is good for kinder to learn that Gott is the one who gives life and the one who decides when our days are done." Greta took the rag and began wiping down the inside of the dessert case. "Of course, it probably helps that our kinder see death regularly, living on farms," Greta said. "They are not like these Englisch children who think that meat comes from McDonald's. Our kinder care for the cow that they will eat. This is part of how they understand that death is part of what it means to live."

Cheryl would have to think about this some more, but she could definitely see the wisdom in what Greta was saying.

"I'm going to the funeral, so I guess I'll see for myself tomorrow," she said, and Greta nodded.

"*Goot.*" She leaned into the dessert case, getting her rag into the far corners. "Now. I am told you are trying to help find proof that Silas owned that land."

"Yes." Cheryl had totally lost count of the money in front of her, so she set it aside and decided to finish that later. For now, she would clean the espresso machine. "The deed that shows Silas owned that land is missing from his files, and the county does not have any record of it."

"I hope you are able to find that deed," Greta said. "It would mean so much to Levi to have his own plot of land." She gave Cheryl a significant look. Cheryl turned before Greta could see her cheeks flush.

"I hope so too. We were trying to open a safe in Silas's office. I'm hopeful the deed is inside there. But we don't know the combination." She thought also of the key Seth had found this afternoon. Would it unlock something that could lead them to the proof they needed?

Greta finished wiping out the display case and rinsed her rag again.

"It seems to me that I always find what I am looking for hiding in plain sight," she said and turned to the sandwiches.

Cheryl almost laughed. If only life were as easy as the aphorism.

"I hope that's the case," Cheryl finally said, shaking her head. "Because at this point, I'm not sure where else to look."

Greta smiled. "Trust in Gott, and He will handle all things."

Cheryl agreed with the sentiment, but she was having a hard time feeling like it was true. Still, she thanked Greta, and together, the two women cleaned the quiet café.

When she got home that night, Cheryl was exhausted, but her mind wouldn't stop spinning. She ate one of the leftover sandwiches from the café for dinner, and then she fed Beau, showered, and crawled into bed.

As tired as she was, it took a while for her mind to stop going back over the events of the day. She thought about Ruthanna Yutzy and what she was hiding. She thought about Bryan Rumble and the disputed border of the land. She thought about the safe in Silas's study, and about the key Seth had found.

She thought about Levi, and about how many people had mentioned to her that it would mean so much to Levi to have land of his own. Cheryl understood this. And yet…

And yet, a small part of her—the base, awful part of her she preferred to ignore—wondered what would happen if Levi didn't get the land. Would that be one less thing tying him to his Amish roots? Might this be God's way of freeing him from the obligation to settle down on a farm and live the Amish lifestyle?

Cheryl felt horrible just thinking it. But there it was. She wished Levi were not Amish. That there was nothing that meant they couldn't be together.

Cheryl rolled over and kicked off the covers. The sad little window unit in this room wasn't cutting it.

She let her mind wander to Naomi and to the funeral in the morning. She wondered what an Amish funeral would be like. She already knew there wouldn't be a lavish coffin and costly floral displays, and she knew there wouldn't be one of those photo collages showing pictures from every stage in his life like there were at so many English funerals. Cheryl had been to short, depressing funerals in tacky funeral homes, and she had been to moving, heartfelt ceremonies held in large sanctuaries packed to the gills with mourners. When her grandfather died, the church had been standing room only and people had lined up down the aisles to say how he had impacted their lives. Which would this be more like? Would family members stand up and talk about Silas?

Cheryl adjusted the pillow beneath her head. Whenever Cheryl heard eulogies at funerals, it made her wonder what people would say about her when she was gone. Would they talk about her smile, her laugh, her fiery temper? How loyal she was to her friends? How much she loved her family? What would Lance say? And Levi?

What would she really want people to say about her?

Cheryl thought for a moment and decided she hoped she would be remembered, first and foremost, for her service to the Lord and then for how her love for Jesus Christ motivated her to love and serve those around her. That's what she wanted them to say.

But was she living in a way that made this likely? Cheryl hoped so. She would need to keep this in mind as she moved throughout her days. What was that saying? Live every day like your last? Cheryl hoped she could do so, keeping her eyes on God.

She rolled over again. Now she was getting maudlin. It definitely wasn't getting her any closer to falling asleep.

Her mind drifted back to the events of the day. Something about that key that Seth had found stuck in her mind. Why did it look like she'd seen it somewhere before?

She climbed out of bed and pulled the key out of her purse and slipped it out of its envelope. It felt heavy in her hand. She couldn't have seen this exact key before, but she felt sure she'd seen one like it. It was a distinctive shape, thin and long.

Cheryl shook her head. Whatever it was that was nagging at her, it was staying just out of reach. She'd try to figure it out in the morning. She slipped the key back into the envelope, tucked it into her purse, and climbed into bed.

Just as Cheryl was finally drifting off to sleep, it came to her. She knew where she'd seen a key like this before.

She knew what that key unlocked.

CHAPTER EIGHT

Thursday morning dawned clear and bright, with just a few high clouds scattered across the luminous sky. Cheryl had slept deeply, but she still wanted to stay in bed. She snuggled under the covers a minute longer, enjoying the changing colors of the sky through the window in her bedroom, but finally, she pushed herself out of bed. She studied her closet for a few minutes.

She was attending an Amish funeral today. She knew what to wear to a regular funeral, but what did one wear to an Amish funeral? Did they all wear black? But they wore black or other somber colors most of the time anyway. Finally, she decided on a navy blue dress and flats, got ready as quickly as she could, threw some food in the bowl for Beau, and headed out the door.

First, she headed to the Honey Bee. She didn't know how Kathy kept up these hours. The first thing she did was make herself a nice big latte with an extra shot of espresso. Then, ready to face the world, she set about getting the little café open for business. Just before eight, Agnes Winslow stepped inside.

"Hello, Cheryl."

"Agnes." Cheryl looked up from setting out the newly delivered bread. Agnes ran the Sisters Quilt Shoppe, which sold quilts, of course, along with fabric and notions. It was a popular spot for tourists. The handmade Amish quilts in the shop were exquisite, each one a result of thousands of hours of careful stitching by women from the area. "Thank you so much for coming."

"Happy to." She pushed back a stray hair that had fallen from her ponytail. "So what do I need to do?"

Cheryl quickly showed her the ropes, making sure she understood how to make the drinks and use the register especially. Though Agnes wasn't Amish, she was older, and Cheryl wasn't sure she would know what to do. But Agnes waved her hand, indicating that she understood. "I can handle this."

Cheryl made sure she knew what to do to hand everything off to Deborah Hoffman, who was married to Jacob Hoffman of Hoffman's Furniture and who would be coming to relieve Agnes in a few hours. Then Cheryl headed out to her car. It was strange not to be going to the Swiss Miss, but she knew Kinsley would have everything under control.

Then she drove out to the Miller farm. Dozens of Amish buggies clogged the roads as she approached the farm, and she had to drive slowly and carefully. She parked as far from where the men were unhitching the horses as she could, and she made her way into the house. There were a few women talking quietly in the kitchen, but most of the people were sitting in silence in the living room. At least, she was pretty sure it was the living room. She'd been in this room dozens of times before, but it looked totally different. The furniture had been removed, and now rows of backless wooden benches were lined up along the length of the room. At the front of the room, a simple pine coffin sat on a low table. Women were seated on one side of a center aisle, the men on the other. No one spoke, and most appeared to be praying silently.

"I am so glad you came." Naomi appeared by her side, whispering. "Thank you."

"I'm glad to be here." She looked out over the quiet room. "But I'm not really sure what I'm supposed to do."

"Go ahead and have a seat." Then, after thinking for a moment, she added, "If you need to use the outhouse, it would be smart to do so now. These services can go on for a while."

Cheryl thanked her friend and took a seat in the second to last row of the women's side. She had noticed that the back row, which was pressed up against the wall, was taken up by older women and heavily pregnant women, and Cheryl realized it was because these were the only seats in the room with backs.

She settled in, trying to take up as little space as possible so she didn't feel so out of place here. She watched as men, women, and children filed in and took seats. Naomi's family sat near the front, and Lydia sat with her mother and sisters. In the middle of the rows of benches, Greta Yoder sat with her daughters and granddaughters over at one side. Cheryl recognized several other Amish people she knew and realized that most of the shops in town must be closed this morning. She easily found Levi, sitting next to his brothers and father, his handsome face stoic. She saw him turn and look at her and then quickly look away, as if embarrassed to be caught. Then, finally, an older man with a long gray beard took his place at the front of the room.

Without preamble, he started speaking in Pennsylvania Dutch. He spoke for a few minutes, and then the whole room went quiet, and Cheryl noticed that everyone around her had bowed their heads and seemed to be praying silently. She remembered that the Amish did not pray out loud like they did at her church. Then, at some signal she didn't understand, everyone stood and began singing. Cheryl didn't recognize the tune, and the words were in a foreign language, but the song was slow and it sounded like a dirge.

One of the older women in the last row tapped Cheryl on the shoulder, smiled, and handed her an open songbook. Cheryl thanked her as she took it, but even looking at the page of words in front of her didn't help. There were no notes, just words on the page, and she didn't understand a bit of what they meant.

Finally, the slowest song in history ended. Everyone sat down, and the man at the front of the room started talking again. Cheryl quickly realized he had launched right into a sermon, seemingly with no notes, but she couldn't follow a word of it. She heard the word "Gott" over and over again, but beyond that, Cheryl was lost. The benches were uncomfortable, too, and she wiggled around, trying to get comfortable, but she noticed that no one else seemed to be having trouble. Even the children were sitting quietly, listening. Children at her church never sat still this long.

She started to zone out as the preaching went on and on—Naomi had not been exaggerating about how the service could go long—but then Cheryl decided to use the time to pray. She prayed for comfort for Silas's family, and she prayed for Aunt Mitzi, that her work would be productive in Papua New Guinea. She prayed for Kathy Snyder and for her mother. And she prayed for Levi and for wisdom as she tried to help him prove that Silas had owned that land. She prayed that God would open the right doors and that they would find the answers they needed—and quickly.

Finally, she realized that the people around her had all stood up and were singing again, and then, suddenly, it was over. Cheryl was bewildered. She hadn't understood much of what was said, but from what she could tell, it had seemed to largely be about God, not about Silas. She hadn't even heard his name mentioned at all, in fact, until the last few sentences. And there were no eulogies, no impassioned and tearful remembrances. It had been all about God.

Cheryl stood up and slowly made her way out of the row of benches, along with the women around her. Cheryl made her way to the front of the room. She had hoped to catch Seth before he left for the grave site.

She saw him talking quietly with a group of men, who seemed to be discussing moving the coffin to the yard. She hesitated. She didn't want to interrupt—but was this important enough that Seth would want her to?

She hesitated, and as she was trying to decide what to do, Levi appeared next to her.

"Thank you for coming," he said quietly. She felt her stomach flop at the sound of his voice—which was completely inappropriate at a funeral, she reminded herself.

"Of course. I was glad to."

"Did you enjoy the preaching?" He gave her a sly grin.

"It was...thorough."

"Not many men could talk for two hours straight with no notes," Levi said, grinning.

"That is true. But from what I could tell, he didn't really talk about Silas at all." Cheryl smiled. "Did he just not like him or what?"

"It is Gott, not Silas, we need to be thinking about always."

He wasn't wrong, she supposed, though it did seem a bit harsh. Still, it wasn't the strangest thing her Amish friends did.

"Hey, I was trying to figure out a way to ask your dad a couple things," Cheryl said. "But I didn't want to interrupt."

Levi looked at his father, who was at the front of the room. The other, younger men around him were grasping the coffin, and Seth was observing. Around them, teenage boys were starting to pick up the long wooden benches and carry them out of the house.

"I will go ask him. What is it you need to know?"

"I wondered if he knew which bank Silas used." Cheryl quickly explained what she'd figured out last night and why she wanted to know, and Levi nodded and said he would ask.

"And can you tell him I spoke with the lawyer Luke Bradshaw, and he is willing to file an injunction to try to block the sale of the land, for free. But he needs to do it today."

Levi nodded and then headed toward his father. Cheryl stood frozen in place as the two men talked quietly. Even if she could have heard what they were saying with all the noise going on around her, they were speaking in Pennsylvania Dutch. Cheryl moved out of the way as two young men grasped the bench she was standing next to.

A few minutes later, Levi walked back to her.

"Daed does not know which bank Uncle Silas used," Levi said. "He thinks the answer is probably in the files at the house, but he cannot go look now. He will try to find out later today."

"And what about the lawyer?"

"He says he will need to talk about the lawyer with his brothers."

Cheryl felt frustration rise. Didn't he realize that time was ticking away and that the sale was tomorrow? If they didn't move to block this now, it would be too late.

Seth said something to Levi from the far side of the room, and Levi nodded and then turned back to Cheryl. "I must go to the cemetery now. But my father asks if you will go to Silas's house at one to let the locksmith in. He will try to crack the safe then."

"Of course."

Levi nodded. "Good. We will go there too after the burial."

She watched as Levi crossed the room in several long strides. She followed a few moments later, thinking she would sneak out quietly so as not to be an imposition, but Elizabeth Miller stopped her.

"Cheryl. You must come meet my uncle Emmon and his family." She took Cheryl's arm and led her through the crowd to the backyard, where a group was standing in a circle near the vegetable garden, talking in low tones.

Cheryl recognized the name belonging to Seth's brother who was to inherit the house and main plot of land from Silas. And she quickly picked him out from the group because he bore a striking resemblance to Seth—he had the same high, strong cheekbones, dark hair, and intense eyes.

"Uncle Emmon, this is mother's friend Cheryl Cooper. She is the one helping us try to prove that Silas owned that land."

"Hello." He nodded at her. "Thank you for your help. My whole family appreciates it." He then introduced the other members of his family, but so many names went by that they all became a blur. Elizabeth talked with her uncle for a few minutes in Pennsylvania Dutch, and then he nodded and said, "I am sorry, I must go hitch up the horse. But I am told the locksmith will be coming back to Silas's house later, and I would like to take a look around as well. Perhaps I will see you there."

With that, he turned to go. Elizabeth apologized and said she had to go too, but she thanked Cheryl for coming.

Cheryl said good-bye and started toward the front of the house, intending to slip away, but as she rounded the corner of the house, she realized she was too late. Most of the mourners at the funeral were already loading up into buggies and hurrying off. The coffin had been loaded onto a wagon, and a line of buggies was slowly making steady progress down the road toward the Amish cemetery. It would be some time before she would be able to get out.

Rover came up, and she nuzzled his head and thought about what to do while the driveway cleared out. There were still people moving around inside the house, and she could hear through the open windows. Cheryl went back around to the rear door and pulled open the screen door. As she stepped in, she saw that the living room had been transformed again, and now the benches were gone and tables were set up down the length of the room. A number of Amish women were bustling around, setting out tablecloths and stacking silverware. This must be the meal Naomi had baked so many pies for. It appeared that a handful of women had stayed behind to set up while the rest of the mourners went to the grave site. They would no doubt return here for the meal after Silas was in the ground.

"Cheryl."

Cheryl turned and was shocked to see Ruthanna Yutzy standing in front of her in Naomi's kitchen, holding a pitcher of water.

"I was hoping you hadn't left yet." Ruthanna looked around the room, set the pitcher on one of the tables, and gestured for Cheryl to follow her. "I saw that you were here, and I wanted to talk to you."

"You were here at the funeral?" How had she missed seeing her? She supposed there had been a number of women, all dressed alike, and from the back, it wouldn't have been hard to miss her, but...Cheryl shook her head, disoriented. After dodging her questions twice yesterday, why would Ruthanna suddenly want to talk to Cheryl?

"Come. I must fill up another pitcher," Ruthanna said, and picking up a metal jug from the kitchen counter, she started toward the back door. Because Cheryl didn't know what else to do, she followed her. Ruthanna crossed the dirt yard and stopped when they were a few feet from the hand pump.

"I'm sorry I blew you off yesterday," Ruthanna said. Cheryl felt her mouth drop open. It wasn't just the words she said, it was the way she spoke—not the formal speech that characterized so much of her interactions with the Amish, but with contemporary slang. "I wanted to be straight with you, but I couldn't, not with my mom there. But she went to the grave site, so we're good, as long as the others don't overhear."

Something was definitely different about the way she spoke now. Cheryl was more confused than ever.

Ruthanna looked around the yard and then, seeing that they were alone, continued. "I promise you, I had nothing to do with that deed disappearing from Silas's files. I didn't even know it existed, let alone have any reason to take it."

"So you didn't date the developer Michael Borland?"

"Oh yeah. I did date him. I'm not disputing that. And I knew he wanted that land. Somehow he even knew that there was some question about the ownership. But I asked him not to pursue it. I asked him not to do anything to cause sweet old Silas to lose his claim to that land."

A strand of her hair was picked up by a passing breeze, and she smoothed it back under her bonnet.

"How did he know there was doubt about the ownership?"

"I don't know. I just know that Michael didn't try to get that land, partly because I asked him not to, and that I had nothing to do with the deed going missing."

Cheryl took this in. It made sense, in some ways. But... "Why didn't you mention any of this yesterday?"

"I couldn't talk about him yesterday because my mom would have lost it. She hates even thinking about that time, and she was still there when you came back last evening, so I couldn't come clean then."

"Why do you talk like that?"

Ruthanna laughed. In retrospect, Cheryl would probably have chosen to rephrase that question, yet it remained.

"I don't know how much Naomi told you, but I didn't join the church until pretty recently. So I had a lot of time to pick up Englisch habits."

"But you didn't talk like this yesterday."

"I know how I'm supposed to act." Ruthanna shrugged. "Anyway, while I was running around, I met Michael, and we started dating. He is a very smart businessman, and he is very young to have accomplished as much as he has. He was a good guy. *Is* a good guy. And I know he would never try to cheat Levi out of his land."

"How can you be sure about that?"

"In the same way you are sure that Naomi didn't steal that deed from Silas's records. You know her and know she would never do such a thing. It goes against her character."

"The difference is, Naomi has nothing to gain from taking that deed. Michael has everything to gain. And you, as his girlfriend, would have had a very good motive to help him out."

"I know it looks that way, but I promise you, that's not what happened. I have never seen Silas's copy of that deed in my life, and I don't know where it is."

It all seemed too convenient, too suspicious, to simply ignore the connections here. If Ruthanna wasn't behind this, it was a heck of a coincidence.

The thing was, Cheryl believed her. There was honesty in her voice and a complete lack of guile that Cheryl found believable. She was either a very good liar, or she really didn't know anything about that deed.

"Anyway, I wanted to tell you that," Ruthanna said. She leaned over and held the pitcher under the waterspout, and with the other hand she lifted the handle on the hand pump. She was very practiced, but it still looked awkward.

"Let me help you," Cheryl said and took the pitcher from Ruthanna's hands.

"Thank you." Ruthanna used both hands to pump the water while Cheryl held the pitcher under the spout. "That's probably the thing I miss most since I joined the church. Indoor plumbing is pretty much the best thing ever invented."

Cheryl had to agree with her on this one. Just the idea of using the outhouse in the middle of the night was enough to give her the willies.

"So here's my question: even if Silas's copy of the deed is missing, shouldn't there be records on file with the city or county or something?" Ruthanna huffed a bit as she pumped the handle up and down. "How can they just pretend that he didn't own the land?"

"That's the strangest part of all of this. The county has no record of anyone owning that parcel of land. The file that should have it is gone." Cheryl jumped a bit as cold water splashed out on to her hand.

"There are no electronic records?"

"It's not there. Either it's been deleted from the records or it was never there to start with."

"Really?" Ruthanna stopped pumping and cocked her head. "Do you know what kind of software they use to store the files?"

"Uh, no." Cheryl looked at Ruthanna, who had her eyes narrowed, her gaze far off. "I didn't ask." She was confused. "Why?"

"There can't be that many kinds of database software that they use. I assume it's password protected, but…" Ruthanna started pumping again, thinking quietly to herself for a few moments, and then she nodded. "I could try to see what happened to that file."

Cheryl narrowed her eyes. "What?"

Ruthanna laughed. "Seriously. Do you want me to try?"

"How in the world would you do that? Aren't you, well, you know…" Cheryl shrugged. "Amish?"

"Oh yes. I can't actually go in and try to find the data myself because I don't own a computer, but I still have friends who can try to find it for me."

Cheryl just stood there, trying to understand what was happening. Could this girl really be serious?

Ruthanna saw the confusion and sighed. "Yeah. Like I was saying, I almost didn't join the church. I really wasn't sure I wanted to be Amish at all. Most of these Amish kids, they don't realize there's a big world out there, so *rumspringa* for them is getting a cell phone, maybe smoking a few cigarettes if they're feeling really naughty. But I wanted more than that. I wanted to get an education. So I did."

"And you became a computer hacker?"

"I was interested in computers. So I got a GED and then enrolled in classes at the community college. I studied computer science, among other things."

Cheryl couldn't believe what she was hearing. Was this girl for real?

"That's where I met Michael. He was teaching classes in business development, and we got talking, and we hit it off." Ruthanna started cranking the hand pump again.

As unlikely as their relationship sounded, Cheryl could almost imagine this. No doubt Ruthanna's good looks had a lot to do with the two of them hitting it off.

"I liked programming. It was like a puzzle. For a while, I considered quitting the church and moving to Silicon Valley."

"But you didn't."

"I didn't."

"But..." Cheryl struggled for words. "You just...gave that all up? To stay Amish?" She didn't want to come out and ask why, but no doubt Ruthanna understood what she was getting at.

Ruthanna shrugged. "I fell in love."

"So you and Michael had broken up."

"Oh yeah. It wasn't a serious thing with him. He's a good guy, and I liked him, but we were just too different. It wasn't going to work. And then when I came home for my sister Kathryn's wedding, I started talking to Daniel, and we just..." She shook her head. "I'd had a crush on him when I was younger, but I wasn't ready. But then, at the wedding, I was."

"So you joined the church."

"I joined the church."

The jug felt heavy in her arms, and she realized water was creeping up to the rim. She started to set the jug down on a stump next to the pump, and Ruthanna stopped pumping. Cheryl tried to figure out how to phrase this next bit.

"Are you glad you did it?"

"I love Daniel."

Cheryl nodded. Ruthanna hadn't really answered the question, but she'd said enough.

"Anyway, when I was taking classes, I made some friends. With programmers. And I still keep in touch with some of them. I think one of them might be able to help."

"They're going to get into the county's systems?"

"They could try."

"Is that legal?"

Ruthanna paused. "It would be in service of righting a wrong, right?"

She supposed that was true, though she wasn't sure she felt comfortable with breaking the law to get what they needed.

"I will make sure they do not do anything wrong," Ruthanna said, and Cheryl felt a little better.

Ruthanna glanced back at the kitchen door. "I should get back inside."

"Of course."

Ruthanna picked up the water jug. "I will let you know if we find anything."

"Thank you." Cheryl saw that the crowd of buggies had cleared, and so she headed toward her car. She should stay out of the way of the women preparing the meal. Besides, she had some errands to run.

First, Cheryl called the shop to see how Kinsley was doing. She answered right away and said that she had everything under control. The girl was a bundle of energy, and Cheryl believed her. Cheryl asked if she minded if Cheryl stayed out for a bit longer. Kinsley didn't mind, so Cheryl thanked her. The driveway was clear now, and she would be able to get out without getting stuck in an Amish traffic jam.

As she walked, she used her cell phone to search for banks in the area. There were nearly a dozen. There was no way to guess which one she should try, so she picked the closest one and set her GPS to navigate there.

As she pulled out of the driveway, Cheryl had to laugh.

Somehow she'd come across what had to be the only Amish computer hacker in the world.

CHAPTER NINE

Cheryl pulled up in front of Central Ohio Savings Bank and stepped in through the glass door. It was built of tan bricks and had acoustic ceilings and a polished tile floor. She walked past the small waiting area, set with worn stuffed chairs, and headed toward the tellers. There was an Amish man in line in front of her. She took that as a good sign.

When it was her turn, she stepped up to the counter and greeted the teller, a young woman in a crisp blazer who had a thick layer of foundation caked on her face plus heavy eye makeup. Cheryl rummaged in her purse until she pulled out the envelope Seth had found in the workshop and slid the key onto the counter.

"I'm trying to figure out if this key opens one of your safe-deposit boxes." Cheryl pushed the key across the counter toward her. "It's box 415."

Cheryl tried to contain her excitement. Last night as she'd lain in bed, she'd remembered where she'd seen a key like the one Seth had found in the workshop before. When her grandfather had passed away, her dad had taken Cheryl with him to retrieve the items he'd kept in a safe-deposit box at the bank. None of it was excessively valuable, but her grandfather had watched a lot of "disaster of the day" news programs and feared someone would break in and steal it all some night, so he had slept better with it safely locked up in the bank. When Cheryl had gone with her father to get Grandpa's things, Cheryl had been fascinated by the rows upon rows of small locked boxes at the bank, and she remembered seeing the distinctive shape of the key that opened his safe-deposit box.

"Huh." The woman picked up the key and looked it over. "Does the box belong to you?"

"Well…" Cheryl started to panic. Would they refuse to help her if it wasn't hers? "Not exactly."

The woman let out a bit of a snort and then shook her head. "I'm afraid I can't tell you anything if you don't own the box."

Cheryl briefly explained the situation, that the owner had died and they were trying to figure out what was inside, but the woman said she wasn't allowed to break the rules, no matter the circumstance. The legal heirs would need to come to the bank with the appropriate paperwork in order to get access to the box.

"And unfortunately, safe-deposit box keys all look pretty much the same, so I couldn't say based on the key whether the box was one of ours anyway."

The teller picked up the envelope the key had come in and turned it over. She looked up, glanced at the man seated behind the desk marked Manager at the far side of the lobby, and turned back to Cheryl. Then she quickly opened a drawer and pulled out a small white envelope. It was the same size and shape as the envelope Seth had found, but it had the words Central Ohio Savings Bank stamped on it underneath the bank's logo. "But I can tell you that *this* is one of the envelopes our safe-deposit box keys come in."

Cheryl understood what the woman was saying without saying. Judging by the envelope, it was unlikely the key had come from this bank. Cheryl thanked her and headed back out to the car.

It would be slow going to try to figure out which bank held the safe-deposit box this key opened, but she would drive to each one if he had to. She wasn't sure what she would do then—it didn't seem like they would let her open the box even if she knew where it was. But still, she had to try.

Cheryl looked back at her phone and picked the next closest bank and then drove there with similar results. By the time she'd been turned away from the third bank, she was starting to feel discouraged. Even if she figured out what bank held the right deposit box, how would she be able to get inside? Seth would no doubt be able to get the proper paperwork lined up to gain access to the box at some point, but she doubted it would happen before the sale went through tomorrow. If the deed was inside this safe-deposit box, they needed to get into it ASAP.

Cheryl felt frustration rise, but there was nothing to be done, and besides, it was time to head over to Silas's house to meet the locksmith anyway. Maybe the deed would be inside that safe after all. In any case, maybe she could find some of his bank records at the house so she wasn't blindly trying every bank in town.

Cheryl pointed her car toward Silas's place, and fifteen minutes later she stepped inside the quiet house. It was unlocked, as most Amish homes tended to be. She was a few minutes early, so she went into the office, sat down at the desk, and looked around.

It had to be in here somewhere; she felt it. The proof that they needed was in this room somewhere. What had Greta Yoder said? That whenever she was looking for something, she tended to find it hidden in plain sight?

She let her eyes wander, taking in the worn wooden floor and the linen curtains that hung in front of the windows. Finally her eyes rested on the cross-stitched verse on the wall. *Beloved, let us love one another.*

Something about that snagged at something in the back of her mind.

Cheryl turned the words over in her mind, thinking them through. The verse came from 1 John. She had learned a little song about it in Sunday school when she was a kid.

Beloved, let us love one another.

Wait a minute. Cheryl jolted up in her chair. What had the locksmith said the first number in the combination was yesterday? Sixty-two?

Cheryl jumped up and ran into the kitchen where she'd seen a worn leather Bible. She quickly flipped to the list of books of the Bible in the front and ran her finger down the list. She got nearly to the end, counting in her head as she went...

That was it. She had it. Cheryl laughed, and then she slammed the Bible shut and ran into the office. A few spins of the dial, and the safe opened.

CHAPTER TEN

Y ou figured out the combination *how?*" Levi looked incredulous, and Seth and Emmon were both looking at her as though she'd told them she'd opened the safe using lasers shot from her fingertips.

The Amish men were standing in the office of Silas's house, staring at the open safe door while Cheryl sat in the desk chair, neatening the piles of papers she'd pulled from the safe.

She'd explained that she'd gotten the safe open shortly before the locksmith arrived, and she'd paid him and sent him away. By the time she'd finished examining everything inside the safe, the Amish men had arrived, having skipped out on the meal following the burial and coming here straight from the cemetery.

"The locksmith had already told us the first number in the combination was sixty-two," Cheryl said. "So when I looked at this picture"—she pointed at the small cross-stitched wall-hanging once again—"and realized that First John is the sixty-second book of the Bible, it wasn't hard to guess what the last two numbers in the combination were."

Emmon still looked confused, but Seth nodded, and Levi said quietly, "Four and seven."

"Exactly." Cheryl nodded. "Sixty-two, four, seven; the sixty-second book of the Bible, fourth chapter, seventh verse. Greta Yoder told me it was probably hidden in plain sight, and she was right."

"Who is Greta Yoder, and how did she know the combination to the safe?" Emmon said.

Levi laughed and shook his head, and Seth said something in Pennsylvania Dutch to him, and he nodded.

"I still do not understand how you thought to try those numbers, but I am so thankful you did," Seth said.

"Unfortunately, after all that, the deed was not inside." Cheryl pointed at the piles of papers she'd stacked neatly on the desk. Most of what was inside was cash, recent intake from his business by the look of it. Cheryl guessed there wasn't more than a few hundred dollars in cash here, but Emmon, who was set to inherit it, nodded approvingly at the pile of bills.

More interesting to Cheryl was the short stack of recent deposit slips from First United Bank of Ohio. It had been on her list of banks to contact, but it was not one she'd visited this morning. Silas had had an account there, if these statements were to be believed, which meant that it was at least worth checking to see if Silas had taken out a safe-deposit box there as well.

"So we are not any closer to finding that deed after all," Levi said. Cheryl could see he was trying not to be too disappointed.

"Well, it wasn't in the safe, but I do have another idea." Cheryl quickly explained that the key Seth had found yesterday was a safe-deposit box key and that with the name of the bank, they could now go there and see if he had rented a box. Maybe, Cheryl suggested, the deed was inside the safe-deposit box. She had no explanation for why Silas would have kept that deed separate from all his other equally valuable important papers, but then she didn't understand a lot of what her Amish friends did. And by all accounts, Silas had been quirky. Not only that, it was the best lead they had to go on at the moment, so Cheryl helped Seth and Emmon gather whatever paperwork they could find to prove they were Silas's heirs, and they all climbed into her car.

"What is that noise?" Emmon asked as she pulled out on to the road. He was in the passenger seat and held one hand over an ear as he struggled to buckle his seat belt.

"Cheryl says there is nothing wrong with her car," Seth said, meeting Levi's eye in the backseat.

"It does not sound like nothing," Emmon said as he finally got the buckle into the holder.

"It's been a busy week, but I will take it to have it looked at soon," Cheryl promised.

"I should hope so." The older man shook his head, and Cheryl had to laugh. These Amish all seemed to be automobile experts, to judge from their reactions to her car. She decided to redirect the conversation. "Were there a lot of people at the cemetery?"

None of the men answered right away, but then Levi spoke up, telling her about how only a few words were spoken at the graveside, and then the coffin was lowered into the grave they'd dug, and they scooped dirt over the hole. A simple gravestone had been ordered.

Silence fell over the car, and Cheryl tried to decide whether to bring up the next subject she needed to ask Seth about. Finally, she decided there was no harm in asking. Really, she was only trying to help.

"Did Levi talk to you about my conversation with Luke Bradshaw?" Cheryl asked.

"Yes," Seth said. "We have not decided whether to hire him or not yet."

"We'd need to let him know as soon as we can, probably this afternoon so he'll have a chance at getting the sale blocked," Cheryl said. Seth nodded but did not say anything. Cheryl felt frustration once again, but she knew getting mad would not convince the Amish man to change his mind. He would have to get there on his own.

"Well, hopefully we will find what we need at the bank. And if we don't for some reason, we can go back to Silas's house and keep looking for hiding places and going through files. It has to be there somewhere."

There was a pause, and then Emmon said, "Melinda wants to start cleaning out the house this afternoon." The two other men nodded, but Cheryl struggled to make sense of his words.

"What do you mean?"

"Since the house now belongs to my brother, his wife is anxious to get it cleaned out," Seth said.

"Oh." Goodness. Cheryl had known he would inherit the house, but she hadn't realized they would move so quickly to take ownership. "Isn't there some time until the estate is settled?" Cheryl asked.

"Yes, but we do not anticipate any holdups," Emmon said. "And since we intend to rent it out, we will need to get it emptied rather quickly."

Cheryl's heart raced. If they started throwing out all of Silas's things, they might accidentally get rid of something that would lead them to the deed—or the deed itself.

"Is there any way she could hold off, at least until after tomorrow?" Cheryl asked.

"I do not know." Emmon sighed. "I will try to get her to."

"You could remind her that having a jail next to the house would not be great for the property value," Seth said sensibly.

"Ach. Yes, this is true." Emmon nodded. "I will see if I can convince her to wait until after tomorrow."

They arrived at the bank a few minutes later. It was housed in an unassuming building at the edge of a shopping center off Route 39. Cheryl and the Amish men all trooped inside. Seth clutched a leather bag that held the papers they'd pulled together.

"Hello," said a middle-aged woman at a front counter. "Welcome to First United Bank. How can I help you today?"

The woman's smile was kind, and her curly brown hair framed her face, creating a kind of halo.

"Hi," Cheryl said, since none of the Amish men answered. "We are trying to find out if a man named Silas Miller had a safe-deposit box here."

"Silas Miller." She looked at the three Amish men standing behind Cheryl and grinned. "Amish, right?"

"Yes." Cheryl nodded. She wanted to describe him but struggled to come up with anything that would set him apart from every other Amish man on the planet. "These are his brothers."

The woman looked at Seth and Emmon, and she nodded. "Yes, I know who he is. He used to come in here a lot. Sweet man."

This was encouraging, and Cheryl felt a bit more optimistic as she told the woman, "He recently passed away, and his next of kin are hoping to get access to the box."

"Oh dear." The woman's face fell. "I hadn't heard. I am so sorry." She looked genuinely sad to hear the news. "He never said much, but he was always so polite and sweet." She looked from Cheryl to Seth, Emmon, and Levi.

"Since he's gone, would it be possible to access his safe-deposit box?" Cheryl asked. "Seth is the executor of his estate, and Emmon is the heir."

The woman turned her head and looked over toward the area of cubicles. "Assuming you have the right paperwork, I'm sure it won't be a problem. I'll need to check in with my boss. Would you please wait for just one moment?"

"Of course."

She slipped out from behind the counter and her low heels clacked on the polished floor as she crossed the room. Cheryl wondered why it was that every bank in the world seemed to have high-gloss floors. Was it so you couldn't run on them, forestalling any would-be bank robbers? Or was there some banking décor code?

"Could you step right this way, please?"

The woman was back, and she was indicating that they should follow her. She led them to one of the cubicles, where a woman in a dark pantsuit, hair pulled back into a severe bun, stood waiting. The nameplate on her desk said Alexandra Goldsmith, Manager. Cheryl was disappointed. The woman at the front desk had been so nice, she'd thought she might be willing to help even if they didn't exactly have all the right paperwork. This woman looked like she was a stickler for the rules.

"Hi. I'm Alex," she said, smiling first at Cheryl then at the men. "Please, have a seat." If she wondered what Cheryl was doing with these three Amish men, she didn't let on.

The woman from the front desk had retuned to the cubicle with two more chairs, and it took a bit of maneuvering, but they managed to line up four chairs opposite the desk.

"I am sorry for your loss," she said, and the men nodded without saying a word.

"I understand you'd like to access the safe-deposit box that belonged to your"—she looked at Seth—"brother?"

Seth had a quiet air of authority about him, and somehow she had figured out that he was the one she needed to talk to. Seth nodded.

"I'm going to need to see the death certificate, as well as a copy of the will that says these men are listed as heirs, and identification."

Cheryl had a moment of panic. She hadn't thought about IDs. They obviously didn't have driver's licenses. Did the Amish use IDs?

But Seth, Emmon, and Levi each reached into wallets and pulled out what looked to Cheryl to be authentic government-issued identification. Seth also pulled a copy of the will from his bag and placed that on the desk by the ID cards.

"We do not have the death certificate yet," Seth said. "My brother only passed away on Monday. We buried him today," he said. "But we must get into his box today."

Levi cleared his throat. "We did bring a copy of the *Budget*," he said, pulling a copy of the Amish newspaper out of his father's bag.

Alex eyed both men skeptically but looked down at the newspaper in front of her. Anyone who lived in the area was familiar with the *Budget*, which just about every Amish family in the area read. It was published every Wednesday, and it contained news and gossip from around the country. In addition to the actual news, people could send in updates on their lives and the newspaper would print them. Cheryl knew that many Amish used the *Budget* as a way to keep up on what was going on with far-flung friends and loved ones.

Levi set the paper on the desk. He had circled something, and Cheryl saw that it was a notice about Silas's passing, as well as the time and date of the funeral. He pushed it across the desk. Alex picked up a pair of glasses from the desk, slid them on, and looked down at it.

Cheryl held her breath. It wasn't an official legally recognized proof of death, but in the Amish world, it might as well be. She didn't know if this English bank manager would see it that way, however.

Finally, she looked up and sighed. "Silas Miller was a good man," she said. "I'm sorry that he's gone."

"You knew him?" Seth asked.

Alex nodded. "I once had him re-cover a chair I'd inherited from my grandmother. He did excellent work, and he did it quickly, at a very fair price." She pulled the glasses off and folded them. "And he used to come in here to access his box every few weeks. Didn't say much, but he was a sweet man. Funny guy."

Funny? Cheryl hadn't known Silas, but she hadn't heard him described as funny yet. And he came in to access his box every few weeks? What in the world? Cheryl had the impression most people seemed to put things into their boxes and leave them there. What could be inside that he needed to check on it that often?

"Do you have the key for the box?" Alex asked. Cheryl nodded and pulled the small envelope out of her purse. "Okay. I'll need you to sign in. What's the box number?"

"415," Cheryl said.

Alex pulled a log book out of her desk drawer and opened it to the right page and then handed Seth a pen. Each of the men signed in, and she compared their signatures on their ID cards and then handed them back.

"Technically, I'm only supposed to let these two into the safe-deposit box area," she said, gesturing at Seth and Emmon. "But given the extraordinary circumstances, I think it will be all right."

Cheryl let out a breath she hadn't realized she'd been holding. She knew it probably would have been fine if Seth and Emmon had gone in on their own, but she was afraid there would be some document or valuable item that they wouldn't recognize as important, and it made her feel better knowing she would be allowed to see what was in the box as well.

"That means I'll need your ID too," she said to Cheryl, and Cheryl signed in and handed over her driver's license. Then Alex nodded.

"If you'll follow me."

Cheryl couldn't believe it. It had worked. They were actually going to be able to see what was in that safe-deposit box. She stood and saw that Levi had an incredulous look on his face.

The woman led them across the lobby to a door, and she swiped a magnetic identification card to open it. She held the door, and they stepped into a room with small locked doors lining the walls, floor to ceiling.

"Box 415 is over here," Alex said and led them to a door about four by six inches. Cheryl handed Seth the key, and Seth inserted the key into one of the slots on the door. Alex used her own key, from a bunch clipped to her waist, to go in the other slot on the door. Then she pulled, and a metal box, about the size of a shoe box, slid out of the wall. Alex lifted the box and carried it to a door on the far side of the room, indicating for them to follow her. They were in a short hallway, and Alex led them through one of the doors that branched off, and they stepped into a room with a table in the middle.

"I'm not sure you're going to find what you're expecting," she said, "but this is where Silas used to sit and review the contents."

She set the box down on the table, turned her key a bit more, and the front of the door popped open.

Cheryl leaned in, craning her neck, trying to see what was inside. Slowly Seth pulled out the first thing in the box.

Was that...?

It couldn't be.

But as Seth turned it over in his hands, she realized that it was.

Cheryl couldn't believe what she was seeing.

CHAPTER ELEVEN

W hat is this?" Seth held a Walkman in his hands, the yellow sport version.

"It's a Walkman. I had one like it in middle school."

That didn't seem to clarify anything for Seth, so Cheryl went on.

"A portable cassette player. You open this up here"—she reached over and pulled the front open, revealing the compartment to slide a cassette into—"and then you push this button to make the tape play."

Seth shook his head and handed the Walkman to Levi. Then he reached back into the box and pulled out a handful of cassette tapes and set them on the table. Cheryl hadn't seen tapes in years. She picked one up and saw that it was The Beach Boys. Cheryl had to work hard to not laugh.

"This is from many years ago," Cheryl said. "I haven't seen a cassette tape in decades." She looked through the other tapes on the table: an early Beatles, the same Backstreet Boys tape Cheryl had loved in junior high, Neil Diamond, some Kenny G, a few Sandi Patty, and Amy Grant. So he'd had some Christian music in here too.

"What is the meaning of this?" Seth turned to Alex, but Alex just shrugged.

"You said he used to come in here regularly and review the contents," Cheryl said. "What did he do while he was here?"

"He would sit right there and listen to music," Alex said, pointing at the chair next to Seth.

Seth looked stricken, and Emmon looked angry. And Cheryl could understand why. Portable music players were, after all, forbidden by their *Ordnung*. Silas had given up such things of the English world when he joined the church. What they had found here, and what Alex had told them, was proof that Silas had secretly been breaking the Ordnung for quite a while, judging by the age of this technology.

"You're saying he used to come in here sometimes and just... listen to music?" Cheryl had to admit that she had found the idea kind of delightful. She loved to picture this crusty old Amish man secretly grooving out to Kenny G. And the lengths he had gone to keep his secret—it was charming. He must have loved this music. It must have brought such joy to his soul. But she knew her Amish friends would not see it that way. In their eyes, this was disobedience to the church, plain and simple.

"That's correct." Alex, too, looked like she was trying to hold back a smile. Cheryl could see now why the women at the bank remembered and liked Silas. They must have thought it was sweet, just as Cheryl did.

"Did you know about this?" Emmon asked, turning to Levi.

"No. Of course not," Levi said, shaking his head.

"He probably wouldn't have tried so hard to get in here today if he'd known," Cheryl pointed out.

Seth said something to Emmon in Pennsylvania Dutch, and then the three men talked quietly for a few minutes. Finally, Seth nodded, pushed the cassettes and Walkman back into the box, and turned to Alex.

"We will deal with this another day, after we have decided what to do about it," he said. Alex nodded and locked the box back up. As she carried it out of the small room into the main room where the boxes were stored, Seth and Emmon trailing right behind, Levi hung back and walked by Cheryl.

"Uncle Emmon thinks we need to tell the Bishop, but Father disagrees," Levi said quietly, explaining to Cheryl what had transpired between the men. "Father thinks that since Silas is gone and there is no way for him to make a confession, there is no point in publicly exposing his sin."

Cheryl understood that the family was now in an awkward position. Technically, they probably should inform the leaders of the church that Silas had not been following the rules he'd agreed to live by. But Cheryl could understand Seth's point—Silas was gone, and it would do no good to publicly mar his memory now. When the Amish broke the rules of the Ordnung, they were required to make a public confession to be accepted back as a member in good standing, but Silas couldn't do that now. She didn't envy them the decisions they would have to make.

"What do you think they're going to do?"

"I do not know. But they are not going to worry about it now. This did not get us any closer to finding the deed, so they are going to wait and focus on that for now and worry about this afterward."

"That's smart," Cheryl said. And it raised a very good point. She'd been so hopeful that the safe-deposit box would hold the proof they needed to show that land was Levi's to inherit, but they were no closer to that, and the sale was now only twenty-four hours away.

Cheryl didn't know where else to look, and she was beginning to lose hope.

After she dropped the Amish men back off at the Miller farm, where people were still bustling around, cleaning up after the meal and loading benches back onto the bench wagon, Cheryl waved good-bye and headed back to town.

Because of the disappointment at the bank, Seth had told her to go ahead and call the lawyer to try to get the sale blocked, so she did that as she drove. Luke said his office had not located the records from the sale of the land to Silas yet, but he promised to try to file the injunction right away. At this point, though, he wasn't sure he would be able to get in front of the judge today. Still, he would try.

Cheryl drove back to town and parked in front of the Swiss Miss. First, she needed to get something to eat. It was already midafternoon, and she was starving. Then she would follow up on the few leads she had: She would try again to talk to Michael Borland, the developer. She needed to see what more she could find out about the disputed border. She was still waiting on the list of names of the people who had accessed the county's paper records, and she hoped that Ruthanna would dig up some information on who had deleted them from the electronic files. If they could get more time at Silas's house, she would continue searching through his files and looking for Betty's hiding spots.

Cheryl crossed the street and walked up the steps to the Honey Bee. Oh dear. The line stretched nearly to the door. At this time of day, well past the lunch rush, there should only be a handful of customers in here. It probably didn't help that many of the Amish-owned businesses were closed today for the funeral, so some of the traffic that would normally have gone to Yoder's Corner had ended up here. But that could not account for the length of the line alone. Cheryl saw that Roxanna Velandria, who ran the art gallery Artistic License, was behind the counter, and she appeared to be pouring an espresso drink. Cheryl stepped quickly to the front of the store and ducked around the counter.

"Hi," she said.

"Oh, hey there." Roxanna looked up, the metal milk jug clutched in her hand.

"How's it going?" Cheryl asked. She eyed the line. The woman at the counter who was waiting for her drink was shifting from one foot to the other, texting furiously. She let out a sigh.

"It's going okay. This is my second try on this leaf."

Cheryl looked and saw that Roxanna was painstakingly trying to create a design in the foam of the latte. Cheryl had seen baristas do this at some of the nicer coffee places she had been to in the city, and it was lovely. But it took time.

"Second try? Do you mean you redid the drink once?"

"Yes, she did," said the woman waiting for her coffee. She wore big sunglasses and a loose, flowy shirt over skinny jeans. Cheryl

got the impression she was from a big city and not used to waiting.
"Just for the design." She rolled her eyes.

"I want it to be perfect. Kathy's drinks are always perfect."

A man halfway down the line gave up and headed out the door.

"I know Kathy appreciates that, but right now we just need to
focus on getting customers through this line. The drinks taste the
same, no matter what the foam looks like." Cheryl leaned over and
looked at the next person in line, a man who looked like he was
about to hit something. He was dressed like a tour bus driver, and
Cheryl knew that they had strict schedules to keep. "What can I
get for you?"

"A ham-and-cheese sandwich, please."

"Coming right up."

Cheryl moved around Roxanna to pull a premade sandwich
out of the case, but Roxanna said, "Hang on, those have been
sitting there for hours. I can make a fresh one."

Cheryl stifled the frustration she felt. "These sandwiches are
perfectly fine. They've only been here for a little while. This is what
Kathy always does."

They did not need to be having this conversation at all, and
especially not in front of the customer.

Roxanna finally snapped a plastic lid on the latte and handed
the woman her drink. Then she moved to the register.

"No charge," Cheryl said, and the woman nodded, like this
was the least she could expect, and turned toward the door.

"Roxanna, we have got to get this line moving," Cheryl said.
She put the sandwich on a plate and rang the man up quickly

while Roxanna started making an iced coffee for the next woman in line. Within a few minutes, they had cleared out the café.

"Whew. Thanks so much for your help." Roxanna used the edge of her apron to wipe up a bit of spilled iced coffee.

"Sure thing." Cheryl poured herself an iced coffee and added milk and sugar. She rang it up and added the money to the till. "I have to get back to my shop now, but if more customers come in, let's try to focus on getting them in and out pretty quickly, okay?"

Roxanna nodded. "Sorry about that. I guess my artistic tendencies got the best of me."

"No problem." Cheryl knew that Roxanna was only scheduled to be here for a little while before Gail Murray from Buttons 'n Bows took over. She couldn't mess things up too badly in that time. "And I know that Kathy appreciates the help, either way." Cheryl held up her coffee as a sort of wave, and then she headed out the door and crossed the street to her shop.

Stepping into the Swiss Miss felt like coming home. The AC was blasting, the shelves were orderly, and Kinsley was ringing up a purchase, laughing with the woman. It was such a big difference from the Honey Bee that Cheryl couldn't help feeling a bit guilty. The girl might be young, but she was capable.

"How did it go?"

"Just fine." Kinsley handed the woman the bag, and she waved as the customer turned to go. "It was busy, but I was able to keep up."

Cheryl thanked her for that. Kinsley didn't know much about the Amish or Amish-made goods, though she'd picked up some knowledge when she'd worked here over Christmas. But she was a hard worker and cute as a button. Cheryl knew she was quite a good salesperson.

"I really appreciate your help."

"I'm so glad you asked. If you need any more help while I'm in town, please let me know."

Cheryl promised to send her a check, and Kinsley peeled off her apron and went out the door. Cheryl rang up a few more purchases, and then she straightened up a bit. There wasn't much else to do at the moment, so she settled down at the counter. First, she tried to call the developer Michael Borland again, but once again the receptionist didn't answer, and it rang and rang until Cheryl gave up.

She logged in to her e-mail and sorted through the spam, the newsletters, and a message from the library reminding her that her books were overdue. And then she saw a name that at first she didn't recognize. Allison Rumble. It took Cheryl a moment to put it together that this was the wife of Bryan Rumble, the Englisher who had sold his land to Silas.

Cheryl clicked on it eagerly.

Dear Cheryl,

I got your e-mail about the farm my husband Bryan and I owned for a short time while we lived in Sugarcreek. I appreciate your message, and I wish I could be more help, but I'm afraid I'm not sure what I can tell you. We moved to the country hoping for a quiet, peaceful life. We didn't know much about farming, just thought we would learn. But it didn't take long for us to realize that the dream we had romanticized was just that—a dream. The reality of living off the grid in the middle of an Ohio cornfield was harsher than either of us expected. We didn't know what we were doing. We were young and it sounded fun, but it wasn't. Our baby was sick from the cold all the time, and we struggled to make ends meet. And I think we also romanticized living among the Amish, but in the end, we weren't part of their community, and they didn't understand us. Our nearest neighbors in fact became quite snippy about the way we planted our garden. In the end, it seemed better just to move back to the city.

As to your question regarding the documents from the sale, I am sorry to say that I don't have those anymore. My husband passed away a few years ago, and I moved with our kids to a small apartment closer to my mother. I purged a lot of things, including old paperwork. I feel certain the paperwork from the sale of that land was among those I tossed. I am sorry I can't be of more help. I do know we sold it to an Amish fellow named Silas who lived on the far side of the field and wanted to add to his holdings. He was nice enough, though I don't remember his last name. Yoder, or something else Amish, probably. You could see if he is still around and whether he has more information for you.

I wish I could do more to help. Please let me know if you have any further questions.

Best,

Allison Rumble

Well. That was fascinating but ultimately unhelpful. Another door closed.

"Cheryl."

Cheryl looked up and was surprised to see Jessica and Jeff Stockton standing at the counter. Jeff was carrying a tote bag weighed down by a stack of papers.

"Hi there," Jessica said. "I brought my pack mule here."

"I see that," said Cheryl.

"That was some article. Nice work," Jessica said.

"What?" Article? Had the article she'd spoken to the reporter about come out?

"You didn't see it? It was in today's paper." Jeff was tugging a newspaper out of the tote bag on his arm.

"No, I didn't. What does it say?"

"It's great." He placed the paper on the counter and spread it out so she could see the front page.

The headline read: *Jail Planned for Land Seized from Amish Farmer.*

Cheryl skimmed the article. It cited Michael Borland as the developer who had been implicated in other land grabs from local Amish farmers, and pointed out the speed with which he had moved once Silas had passed away, as well the underhanded way plans for the jail had been moved forward. Cheryl was quoted, as were some neighbors in the area of the proposed jail, and there was a photo of her, obviously one lifted from her Facebook page. The article ended with a call for readers to contact the county in an effort to stop the jail from being built in their midst.

"Wow," Cheryl said. "That's great."

"You bet it is. And the phones have been ringing off the hook all day in my office," Jeff added. "People have really responded and are calling to register complaints about the idea of a jail going in. There are even talks of a protest being organized."

"Great." Cheryl couldn't believe it. It seemed like this could really change things. "So are they going to stop the process?"

"Well..." Jeff's voice trailed off. "Not yet. So far it's mostly seemed to annoy my bosses. But that doesn't mean it won't. If enough people raise enough of a fuss, it has to have some effect."

Cheryl hoped so.

"In the meantime, I wanted to bring you this. I pulled the list of people who signed in to access the hard copies of the property records, like you asked. People have to sign in and give their information just so we have it on file before they can look at the records." Jeff slipped the tote bag off his shoulder and set it down on the counter. He slipped the papers out, and Cheryl saw that it was a computer printout with names and other pertinent information for about half a dozen people on each page, and it was about an inch thick. "This is the list of people who accessed the files in the last three months. If you want me to go back further, I can do that, but I thought this would be enough to get you started."

"Goodness. I had no idea this many people accessed the county's property records."

"It's mostly real estate lawyers pulling records to cross the t's and dot the i's when they're working on a sale," Jeff said. Cheryl glanced down at the first page and saw that he was right. "But there might be something useful in there."

"I hope so. Thank you so much for bringing it in," Cheryl said. She didn't know what to look for, but she was hoping some name would jump out at her as suspicious. These pages didn't appear to list which specific property records the people accessed.

"No problem," Jeff said. "Any luck finding the owner's copy of the deed?"

"I'm afraid not." Cheryl shook her head. "And the sale is supposed to go through tomorrow, unless we can get a judge to block it before then."

"Goodness. This developer really must have friends in high places." Jessica shook her head.

"Please let me know what I can do to help," Jeff said.

"This is a good start." Cheryl tapped the stack of papers in front of her. "I really appreciate it."

"Anytime." The two turned and headed out of the shop. A few customers came in, and Cheryl helped them pick out souvenirs for their grandchildren, and then her cell phone rang. She reached for it and saw that it was Luke Bradshaw calling.

"Hi, Luke." Her heartbeat sped up. Maybe he had some good news.

"Hello, Cheryl. I saw the article in the paper this morning."

"Isn't it fantastic?"

He paused. "As your lawyer..."

"Technically, you're not my lawyer."

"As the lawyer working on this case, I should tell you that you shouldn't have talked to the press about this."

She heard what he was saying. But she also heard what he wasn't saying.

"But what about the part of you that's not a lawyer? Aren't you pleased?"

"I am not able to speak about that at this time."

He didn't have to. She could hear it in his voice. He was happy about the piece.

"I'm hoping it will get people's attention," Cheryl said.

"I'm sure it will do that." He sighed, but again, he didn't sound frustrated. "Just don't talk to any more press, okay?"

"All right," Cheryl said. She hung up, and as she set her phone down, she was surprised to see that it was time to close. She had spent almost no time in the shop today. Still, it hadn't been a bad day if the receipts were to be believed. Kinsley had done well.

She cleaned out the register, took out the trash, and straightened things up. Then Cheryl realized that she had a little while before she needed to go over to help close up the Honey Bee. She sat down on the stool behind the counter and pulled over the stack of papers Jeff and Jessica had brought her. She removed the binder clip that held the pages together and scanned through each page, looking for . . . well, anything that looked off, she guessed. As Jeff had said, it looked to be mostly real estate lawyers—or their paralegals—who had accessed the files in recent months. There were a handful of names that didn't appear to be tied to a company, and Cheryl used her laptop to look for information about them, but she didn't pull up anything that looked suspicious. Cheryl returned the papers to a neat stack and put the binder clip back on.

But then, there was nothing to say that whoever had taken the deed from the county records had done so within the last three months. Silas had bought that land ten years ago. It was unlikely anyone had checked to see if the records were still there in that time. Which meant that the deed could have disappeared any time in the last ten years. It would take her forever to go through that many pages of records.

How else could she figure out who had taken it?

But then Cheryl realized there was one person who had access to the files who wouldn't have been listed there. Cheryl got on her laptop and typed in the name of the clerk who oversaw the files, Carolyn Caldwell. But just as results started to show up on her screen, the phone rang. Reluctantly, Cheryl pulled herself away from the screen and grabbed the handset.

"The Swiss Miss, Cheryl speaking."

"Cheryl? This is Gail Murray. I'm at the Honey Bee, and I think a pipe just broke. I can't get it to shut off."

"What? Where is the pipe?"

"Under the sink. It's . . . Cheryl, it's leaking a lot. It's overflowing the bucket I set out. What do I do?"

"Get another bucket. I'll be right there."

Cheryl scrolled through her cell phone and found the number of a plumber she had used when the washing machine at Aunt Mitzi's house had leaked this winter, and she called him. He promised to come over right away. The next call she made was to Roxanna Velandria. Roxanna's gallery, Artistic License, was housed in the basement of the same building as the Honey Bee.

"Roxanna? Cheryl Cooper here."

"Hi, Cheryl. What's going on?"

"There's a pipe leaking in the Honey Bee. I'm sorry to ask this, but where is the water shutoff for your building? Would it inconvenience you terribly if I shut it off, at least until the plumber gets there?"

"Shutting the water off would inconvenience me a whole lot less than water dripping through the ceiling. The shutoff is in the basement. I'll go turn it off now."

"Thank you so much." Cheryl felt her shoulders release. "I'll be right over."

"Thank you for calling."

Cheryl wondered if she should call Kathy to let her know what was going on. But then she decided that Kathy had enough to worry about just now. Cheryl could take care of this, and she'd tell Kathy about it when she was home. She and Kathy could work out the plumber's fee later.

A few minutes later, Cheryl and Roxanna were helping Gail sop up as much water as they could with the stack of hand towels they'd found in the closet.

"I'm so sorry, I don't know how it happened," Gail was saying, pushing a sodden rag across the wooden floor. "I was just washing the dishes, and suddenly water was just pouring out. I don't know what I did wrong."

Gail was an attractive woman in her fifties, and she was always very well-dressed and carefully styled. It was almost funny to see her now in her pressed trousers and silk blouse, scrubbing at the floor. Cheryl knew Gail had had her trials in life, but she couldn't imagine a dirty floor ever having been one of them.

"It could have been something I did when I was in here this afternoon," Roxanna said. She picked up a water-logged box of latex gloves that had been under the sink and tossed it in the trash.

"My guess is it isn't anything anyone did, just a bad pipe and bad timing," Cheryl said. "But we'll see when..."

The front door opened, and Cheryl pushed herself up so she could see over the counter. Curtis Wallace, the plumber, came striding in.

"Speak of the devil," Cheryl said.

"You called?" Curtis laughed. He was a big man with pink cheeks, thinning hair, and an easy laugh.

"Thank you for coming so quickly." Cheryl wrung her rag out into the bucket under the sink and gestured for him to come around behind the counter. His heavy brown work boots thumped on the wooden floor as he walked, and a moment later he was crouched down in front of the pipe. His boots were in a small puddle of water, but he didn't seem to care.

"Yep, you've got a lot of corrosion right here." He shined a flashlight at the pipe and nodded, though Cheryl couldn't see what he was pointing at. It just looked like a pipe to her. "The good news is, it would have happened at some point anyway, so it's no one's fault. The bad news is, it happened today."

Hearing that it was no one's fault made Cheryl feel better, and she could see Roxanna and Gail both exhale as well.

Then he stood, his knees cracking, and turned on the faucet. Nothing came out.

"Is the water shut off?"

"Sure is. Roxanna shut it off. She owns the art gallery downstairs, and she shut it off for us." Cheryl gestured at Roxanna, who pushed a strand of hair out of her face with her forearm and nodded.

"Good." He crouched back down and studied the pipe again. Then he looked at the clock on the wall. "I don't have this size of pipe in my truck. I'll have to go to the hardware store and pick one up. They should still be open, so I can go now and get this fixed up tonight."

"That would be wonderful. Thank you."

He nodded, and without much delay he headed out. Cheryl insisted that Roxanna and Gail both head home, that she would finish cleaning up. Both argued that they would stay and help, but Cheryl won. She'd taken on the task of running the Honey Bee, and she would see it through. She thanked them both for their help today, and as they left, she got to cleaning.

An hour and a half later, her wallet two hundred dollars lighter, Cheryl finally pulled into her driveway. She was exhausted, and the day had taken a turn for the worse when she'd gotten a call from Luke Bradshaw just as she was about to leave the Honey Bee. The judge had gone home early today, so he hadn't been able to get the sale blocked. Luke would try again in the morning. Cheryl had hung up feeling defeated. It had been a long day, and all she wanted to do right now was to shovel some food in and go to bed. But as she was cleaning up after a quick dinner of leftover lasagna, she heard a familiar noise coming from her laptop, which was in the living room.

She ran into the living room and saw the icon for Skype on her screen. Aunt Mitzi was calling!

Cheryl answered the call eagerly, and she felt a rush of emotion as her aunt's beloved face appeared on her computer screen.

"Hello there, Cheryl. How's it going?"

Her aunt's soothing voice was like a balm for her soul. Aunt Mitzi, her father's sister, had been a trusted confidante for many years, and when she had accepted the Lord's call to move to Papua New Guinea, she had asked Cheryl to move to Sugarcreek to take over the Swiss Miss and live in her home. Cheryl, fresh off a breakup with her no-good fiancé, had been thrilled to start a new life in this haven of a small town, and she would always be grateful to Aunt Mitzi for the opportunity.

"Things are good here. How are you? What's going on in your part of the world?"

"It's a beautiful day," Mitzi said. Cheryl could see she was wearing a loose T-shirt over a colorful printed sarong. "I've just been on a long walk with one of my neighbors, and I decided to call my favorite niece to check in. All in all, I'm doing all right. How's Beau?"

"Ah. I see who you really wanted to check in on."

"I called to talk to you. Beau's not much of a conversationalist."

"He's pretty much only good at sleeping. That's what he's currently doing." Cheryl turned the computer so her aunt could see the Siamese cat, currently sprawled out on the couch. "Beau, say hi to Mitzi."

The cat opened his eyes a bit, lifted his head, and decided it wasn't worth the effort. He lowered his head and went back to sleep.

"Good to see he hasn't changed," Aunt Mitzi said.

"Not much around here has."

"It's Amish country. Things do tend to move pretty slowly. But tell me how you are."

"Things are going okay."

"Just okay?"

Where did Cheryl even begin? "It's been a strange few days."

"I almost got rammed by a goat this morning. You can't scare me with strange. Tell me what's going on."

Cheryl laughed, and then she took a deep breath and told her aunt about Silas and the missing deed and how Levi wouldn't inherit the land if they couldn't find proof Silas had owned it before three o'clock tomorrow.

"That would be a big disappointment for Levi, wouldn't it?" Mitzi asked.

"Yes, I think it really would."

"And for you as well." Even from halfway across the world, she could see that her aunt was fixing her with a questioning gaze, asking more than she was really asking.

"Yes, I suppose I would be disappointed as well."

Aunt Mitzi nodded. "Even from the other side of the world, I can see the attraction between you two, clear as day."

Cheryl felt her cheeks burn. Sure, she'd felt herself drawn to Levi, and Levi to her. And she knew other people had noticed it as well. But it was rare that someone came out and said something about it, mostly because it was so...

"It's complicated," Cheryl said.

"Yes, I would imagine it is." There was a rooster calling on Mitzi's end of the line and then the sound of a door slamming. "Falling in love with an Amish man is not exactly simple."

"I'm not in love with an Amish man."

"Well, you're on your way. And after what happened with Lance, I say good for you."

"I'm not..."

"And I know Levi isn't exactly the kind of guy to take this stuff lightly. He's not up for casual dating."

"We're not..."

"I know you're not dating. Goodness, girl, I lived among the Amish for enough years to know that. I know they don't condone an Amish man dating an English girl. And I also know that if you don't stop interrupting me, I'm going to have to complain to my brother that he never taught you any manners."

Cheryl laughed reluctantly. Her parents had always been big on politeness. "Sorry, Aunt Mitzi. Please go ahead."

"It's good to see that threatening to tell your parents still puts the fear of God in you." Aunt Mitzi was smiling, and Cheryl couldn't stop herself from doing the same. Her aunt could be bossy, but she appreciated her. "Anyway, like I was saying, I know the Amish, and I know that even though you and Levi want to be together, there aren't a lot of options. Even just to date you, he would get in trouble, and to get married, he would have to abandon his home, his family, his faith—everything. But I don't see you becoming Amish anytime soon either."

Cheryl sighed. Aunt Mitzi had pretty much summed it up right there. There wasn't any way for them to be together, which was why...

"I know it looks like there's no way for you two to be together," Aunt Mitzi said. "Which is why you are working so hard to deny that you're falling in love with him. It feels safer that way, if you don't admit it." She gave Cheryl a significant look.

Cheryl wanted to argue, but instead she just nodded.

"Well, I know something about the Amish, but believe it or not, I know a thing or two about love as well."

"I know. You and Uncle Ralph were married forever."

"Forty years." For a moment her voice was a bit wistful, and Cheryl was afraid Mitzi would tear up thinking about her husband, who had passed away over four years ago. But then her aunt continued. "Yes, I loved your uncle Ralph, but he wasn't the first man I loved."

"Really?" Cheryl had never heard this before.

"When I was young, before I met your uncle Ralph, I fell head over heels for a man from, well, from the wrong side of the tracks, I guess you could say."

"There weren't literally train tracks separating you, right?"

"It's just an expression, Cheryl." Aunt Mitzi shook her head, like she couldn't believe how dense her niece was, but she was smiling.

"Just checking. I want to understand."

"Well then, stop interrupting." The rooster crowed again on her end of the line. "Anyway, I met Antonio through a friend of a friend, and we just..." Mitzi broke off, and for a moment she was far away. "It was instant. I've never had that kind of immediate attraction with anyone else in my life. I just loved being around him. I thought he hung the moon." That wistful tone crept into her voice again. "But obviously there were challenges, right from the very beginning."

"Like those train tracks."

Mitzi pretended she hadn't heard. "His family thought I was too uppity."

"Uppity?"

"Are you going to let me finish or not?"

"Sorry. Go on."

"My parents about died when they met him. He had tattoos on his arms, and he smoked. He rode a motorcycle."

Cheryl had to laugh. Her aunt was basically describing the bad boy in every teen angst movie ever made.

"He was flaky too, always showing up later than he said, cancelling dates at the last minute, that kind of thing. But then he always brought me flowers or some small gift, and he seemed so genuinely thoughtful, I just forgave him."

"So what happened?"

"It didn't work out, obviously. We were too different, and as much as we wanted to overcome those differences, we just couldn't. He broke things off, and I was heartbroken. But then I met your uncle Ralph, and, well, you know how that turned out."

"Was this story somehow supposed to make me feel better? I don't see how this makes things better with Levi."

"Hush now. I'm getting to that. My point was, things didn't work out with Antonio, but because of him, I knew what I was looking for when the right man did come into my life. I knew that attraction wasn't enough, that I needed to find a man who was solid, dependable, trustworthy. And when Ralph showed up, I recognized him as the man I had been looking for."

"So…" Cheryl tried to understand what her aunt was getting at here. "You're saying after Levi I'll find a guy I'm more suited to?"

"No." Mitzi shook her head. "You know, for someone as smart as you are, you sometimes miss what's right in front of your face." She smiled, and Cheryl knew her aunt was just teasing, so she motioned for her to go on. "I'm saying that after what you went through with Lance, you should be able to see that Levi Miller is everything you want in a man."

"Except that he's Amish. So we're back to square one. Either I become Amish, which, well, that would never work, or Levi leaves the church, which would not only tear him apart from his home and his family but also break the heart of my best friend. So either way, it doesn't work out."

"That's my point, Cheryl. You're only looking at those two outcomes. But there may not only be those two choices."

"How?"

Aunt Mitzi paused. "Have you asked God about it?"

"You mean, have I prayed about the Levi situation? Yes. Every day. I ask Him to take away my feelings for him if we can't be together."

"And has God answered that prayer?"

Cheryl hesitated. "No."

"Didn't think so. Don't stop praying for that, but also, maybe you're not praying for the right thing."

"What do you mean?"

"Have you asked God to show you a third way? A way that you and Levi could be together, even with your differences?"

"No," Cheryl said falteringly. "Does such a way exist?"

"I don't know. I guess that's up to God to decide." Mitzi laughed. "I do remember hearing about some star-crossed couples that ended up joining a Mennonite church. From what I understand, that's usually close enough to Amish that the Amish don't shun members who go that direction. And it's not so extreme that a normal person couldn't do it—most groups use electricity and cars and such. I don't know what the specifics would look like or what the rules about joining the Mennonite church are or whether Levi would even consider it. But I do know that God knows all of those things and more. And I bet if you ask Him, He will guide you as you think about it."

Cheryl's mind was swirling. Become Mennonite? She hadn't considered that. Could that really be a solution? Would Levi even consider it? Did he even want to consider spending his life with her? Cheryl knew they weren't at the stage where they could talk about things like that yet. But she also knew that Aunt Mitzi had just opened her mind to possibilities she hadn't known existed. And she knew that, regardless, her suggestion to pray about it was spot-on. Maybe with Levi it didn't have to be all or nothing.

"You know, you're pretty good at this church stuff. Maybe you should make a career out of telling people about God," Cheryl joked to lighten the mood.

"I'll consider it." Aunt Mitzi winked. "Now, you need to get to bed, and I need to go kill that rooster."

"You're not literally about to go kill a chicken, are you?"

"Goodness no. What happened to you, Cheryl? You didn't used to take everything literally. When did you lose your sense of humor?"

"When your jokes stopped being funny."

"*Humph.*" Mitzi shook her head. "Kids these days. So ungrateful."

"Thanks for chatting, Aunt Mizti. I really appreciate it."

"The pleasure is all mine. Talking with you makes my heart glad." With that, Aunt Mitzi signed off, and her face disappeared from the computer screen.

Cheryl sat there for a few more minutes, looking at the blank computer screen. Was there really any way for her and Levi to have a future together? Could they possibly find, as her aunt put it, a third way? Cheryl knew her faith was the most important thing in her life, and if she ever got married, faith would be the cement that held her marriage together. But she didn't know much about the Mennonites. Was there any way she could be Mennonite? What about Levi?

One thing Cheryl knew for sure was that if she and Levi could find a way to make a life together, having that piece of land would be a huge help. So even though she ached for her bed, she wanted to do one thing first.

She closed the window for Skype and opened up a browser window and typed the name *Carolyn Caldwell* into the search field. She hadn't had a chance to finish the search she'd started earlier, and the clerk was the person who had had the freest access to the county records.

The first thing that popped up for the name Carolyn Caldwell was a social media page. Cheryl clicked on it and was soon scrolling through photos, mostly from family gatherings and a lot of photographs of a boxer puppy named Bernadette. It was a cute puppy, Cheryl had to agree, but there seemed to be an unnecessarily large number of pictures of it. She scrolled down, hoping for something, anything useful. And then...

Cheryl sucked in a breath. It couldn't be, could it?

CHAPTER TWELVE

Cheryl clicked on an image from Carolyn Caldwell's Facebook page to enlarge it, and she stared at the face in the photo. It showed Carolyn with her arm around a younger man wearing jeans and a Dartmouth T-shirt. The caption read, "Me and my little brother, Michael." The last word was highlighted, which meant she could click on it. It was the same guy from the beach photo. The one she'd seen on Michael's own Facebook page.

Which meant that Carolyn Caldwell—she scrolled up to the top and saw that her full name was Carolyn *Borland* Caldwell—was the developer's sister.

Which gave her a very good reason to want to make that deed disappear.

Cheryl really needed to talk to Michael Borland, and soon. She clicked over to his page and studied it, but she couldn't find any way to get ahold of him short of sending him a message. Considering he'd been avoiding her phone calls, she didn't think it was likely he would respond well to a social media message.

She clicked around the site for a while longer, but she wasn't getting anywhere, and she felt ready to collapse, so she shut down her computer and went to bed. She'd have to finish this in the morning.

Cheryl sat up in bed. What in the world was that noise? She looked around, searching for the source of the disturbance, and then she relaxed, realizing it was just her alarm. Goodness. She'd slept like the dead. But instead of feeling refreshed, she felt heavy, languid. But, she thought, pushing the covers aside, it was time to get up. As much as she wanted to go back to sleep, she had to go in and open up the shop, and she had to check in on the Honey Bee, and—she looked at the clock—she only had eight hours until the sale of the land was scheduled to go through. She needed to find that deed, or find some other way to prove that Carolyn Caldwell had stolen the county's copies.

She did her devotions, dressed quickly, tossed some food in Beau's bowl, and headed out to her car. It was already steamy, and Cheryl cranked up the air-conditioning. First, she went by the Honey Bee to open up. Cheryl was feeling like she was starting to get the hang of things around the café, and Tillie Gleason, who ran Amazin' Corn with her husband Bob, came in to help out as planned, but things quickly derailed.

The pastries weren't delivered as scheduled, and when Cheryl called the company to find out why, she was told that they hadn't paid for the pastries for the past few days. Cheryl also discovered that in the madness of last night, she hadn't taken the trash bins out, and now the whole place smelled like garbage. In addition, a quick check of the fridges showed that they were out of milk.

Tillie made a quick run to the big chain grocery store out on Route 39, which was the only place open at this hour, and came back armed with gallon jugs of milk and waxy looking croissants and tough bagels. Cheryl arranged them as best she could in the pastry case, trying to make them look appetizing, and then wished Tillie luck and headed over to open up the Swiss Miss. Cheryl was starting to really appreciate how much easier it was to run her little shop than the café.

Cheryl got things ready to open for the day. Naomi called to let her know that Seth and Levi were going to spend the morning at Silas's house, looking for anything that might point them in the right direction. Cheryl would probably head over there as well at some point, but first she had to get things set up here. Being a Friday in the summer, there would no doubt be many tourists around today.

Cheryl was surprised and grateful when Lydia showed up for work early.

"You just love work so much you can't stay away, huh?" Cheryl asked, counting out cash to open the register.

"Yes. And I love the air-conditioning." Lydia ruffled her skirt, and she stood in front of the vent high on the wall.

Cheryl couldn't even imagine not having any air-conditioning on a day like today. Most Amish houses she'd been in were well ventilated, with windows and doors situated to catch the passing breezes, but it wasn't the same.

Right at ten, a busload of visitors disgorged in front of the shop. Cheryl spent the next hour ringing up purchases of cheese, jam, maple syrup, handmade pot holders, and quilted place mats. But though her hands were busy, her mind was far away, thinking about Silas, about Carolyn Caldwell, about Michael Borland, and about Levi.

She was so distracted that she was surprised when someone called her name. She looked up to find Ruthanna Yutzy standing in front of her.

"Oh, hi, Ruthanna." Cheryl's heartbeat sped up. Had Ruthanna found something?

"Hey. My husband is at the furniture store, and I told him I needed to buy something." Ruthanna looked around, but she saw that Lydia was only a few feet away, restocking the jams. "Can we go outside for a minute?"

"Sure thing." Cheryl took off her apron and gestured for Ruthanna to follow her out the back door. A wave of heat hit her as she stepped outside. They stayed in the shade at the back of the building.

"I talked to some of my friends," Ruthanna said. "And my buddy Shadow was able to get into the county's system."

"Shadow?"

"That's not his real name, obviously." She smirked. "Anyway, he was poking around in the deleted files..."

"But they're deleted. How could he look at them?"

"Nothing is ever really deleted when it comes to computer networks. There's almost always some traces left behind."

"Whoa."

"That's why your IT guy should be your best friend."

"I don't exactly have an IT guy," Cheryl said.

Ruthanna laughed. "Me either." She swished her skirt, trying to catch a breeze. Cheryl was thankful she didn't have to wear heavy long skirts on a day like today.

"Anyway, Shadow found the file. The one that had been deleted."

"So he knows *when* it was deleted?"

Ruthanna nodded. "It was more than two years ago. Someone was planning ahead."

Interesting. So someone might have had their eye on the property as long as two years ago. Who would have been planning that far ahead?

"Better yet, he was able to get the MAC address of the computer that deleted it."

"The what?"

"The MAC address." Ruthanna sighed. "That stands for Media Access Control. Every computer has a unique MAC address. It's like its social security number, or DNA, or something." She looked to see if Cheryl was following. Cheryl nodded. "Every time a computer accesses the Internet, it leaves a fingerprint, so to speak. So when he found the deleted file, he was also able to get the MAC address of the computer that was used to delete it."

"Okay…" Cheryl's mind was spinning. "So can that MAC address tell us who did it?"

"It took some more poking around…"

Cheryl didn't even want to think about what exactly "poking around" entailed. Better not to ask, so she wasn't culpable.

"...but he was able to find the name of the person the computer was registered to. It was"—she reached into a hidden pocket on her dress and pulled out a slip of paper—"Carolyn Caldwell."

Cheryl's heart jumped. There it was. Proof that the clerk had deleted the file. No doubt she'd known her brother was interested in that piece of land and had destroyed the files so her brother could swoop in and get the land for under market rate when it became available. Cheryl wondered if Carolyn was set to get a cut of the money he would make from developing the property.

"That's Michael's sister," Cheryl said.

Ruthanna nodded. "I did not believe it at first. It does not seem like the Michael I knew. But I do not see how she could have destroyed the deed without him knowing." Ruthanna seemed genuinely sad. "I thought he was better than this."

Cheryl was sure he was a nice guy, just like Ruthanna thought, but nice guys did bad things all the time. Being nice didn't mean he wasn't involved.

"How well did you know his sister?"

Ruthanna shrugged. "I met her a few times. She was nice enough, I guess. I don't know. She had some troubles when she was younger, I gathered. Black sheep of the family, that kind of thing. That's why she works for the county instead of running a company like Michael. Their father pulled some strings to get her the job, and she's never found anything better."

Or anything that gave her access to important files like this one did, Cheryl thought. She had to be getting a cut from whatever

Michael made on the land. They'd worked out some kind of scheme. Cheryl wondered if this was the first time she'd pulled this, or if the land deals that had ripped off the Amish in the past had been orchestrated by them in a similar way.

"The problem is, I don't know what you can do with this information," Ruthanna said.

"What do you mean?"

"Well, I'm not sure information like this is . . . exactly admissible in court."

Ah. Cheryl understood what she was getting at. The information hadn't been obtained, well, in a totally legal way. Which would mean they wouldn't be able to use it in court, never mind the fact that Ruthanna's friend—and Ruthanna—would get in trouble if she tried.

"No, I suppose it can't." Cheryl thought for a minute. Maybe she couldn't use this information, but in any case, she needed to talk to Luke Bradshaw. Maybe he could find a way to use this information to get the judge to postpone the sale. And maybe now that she had proof—whether she could share it or not—that Michael was involved, he'd finally have to talk to her.

"Do you happen to know how I would get ahold of Michael?" Cheryl asked.

"It's Friday. He always plays squash at the Health and Racquet Club in Canton on Friday mornings. At least he did when I knew him. I would guess he still does. What time is it?"

"It's just after ten."

"You may be able to catch him if you go now."

"Thank you so much, Ruthanna," Cheryl said. "I really appreciate it."

The girl nodded, and the strings of her kapp bobbed. "And I would appreciate it if it didn't get out that I was still in touch with my old friends."

"Of course. My lips are sealed." Cheryl couldn't even begin to imagine how much trouble it would cause Ruthanna if it came out that this sweet Amish wife was keeping in touch with her hacker friends. Just the thought was enough to make Cheryl laugh.

Ruthanna went back inside, and Lydia rang up her purchase of a jar of jam so her husband would see that she had bought something, and she exited the shop, her long skirt swishing as she walked. Cheryl followed a bit behind and hopped into her car. She set her GPS to navigate to the Health and Racquet Club, and then while she drove, she picked up the phone and dialed the cell phone number Luke Bradshaw had given her.

When he picked up, he explained that he was waiting at the courthouse to try to get in front of the judge, but he had a backlog of cases and it was slow going. Luke wasn't sure he'd be able to get the sale put off.

"But you have to. Wait until you hear what I found out."

Cheryl quickly filled him in on how the electronic records had been deleted by a computer registered to Carolyn, the developer's sister and clerk.

"How did you get this information?" he asked.

Cheryl decided to evade the question. "Don't you see? The fact that it was deleted means it had to have been there in the first place," she said. "The paperwork was legally filed. The land belonged to Silas."

"That may well be, but if I don't have legal proof of this, it doesn't really do me any good."

"Can't you tell the judge, as part of the case for blocking the sale?"

"If this information was obtained illegally, then no, I really can't," he said. Cheryl felt like screaming. They were getting so close, and yet actually putting a stop to the sale seemed so distant.

"What is that noise? Is that your car?"

"It's fine. It's nothing to worry about. I'm getting it checked out."

"I hope so. Goodness."

"So do you think you'll be able to get in front of the judge?"

"I will do my best, Cheryl. And by the way, that article you were quoted in has caused quite a ruckus down here at the county office. People are in an uproar over how this whole jail thing went down. There have to be two dozen people protesting outside."

"That's fantastic!"

"It would be more fantastic if they could actually get in here to make their voices heard, but the security guards are making them stay outside. Still, it's something."

"Maybe it will make a difference."

"Let's hope so." He sighed. "And I'll keep trying, I will promise you that," he said, and Cheryl knew that it would have to be enough. There wasn't anything else to do. "In the meantime, you keep trying to find Silas's copy of that deed," he told her. Cheryl promised she would and hung up.

Cheryl's GPS told her she was getting close to the Health and Racquet Club so she slowed down and scanned for it. Ah. There. It was housed in a tall, stately brick building set back from the road and shaded by arching trees.

Cheryl pulled into the parking lot and quickly located Michael Borland's BMW—the MikeyB vanity plate was a dead giveaway. Cheryl parked her car and stormed over toward his, stopping on a small grassy divider. She would wait here.

She only had to wait a few minutes, however, before he came out of the building. Cheryl recognized him immediately from the Facebook pictures. His close-cropped hair and high cheekbones made him quite attractive. He wore a well-tailored three-piece suit, and he had a gym bag slung over his shoulder, his cheeks pink and his hair wet. He didn't notice her until he had popped the trunk and was about to sling his bag inside.

"Michael Borland?"

He looked up and noticed her for the first time.

"My name is Cheryl Cooper, and I have proof that your sister Carolyn Caldwell is helping you illegally obtain the land belonging to Silas Miller."

"I'm sorry...what?" He let the bag fall into the trunk gently. He didn't seem indignant, just confused.

"The land you're trying to buy? The sale you're rushing through before anyone can prove that the land actually *did* belong to Silas Miller? I have proof that your sister is helping you steal it."

"You're that lady from the newspaper article, aren't you?" He stared at her. "Look, I don't know what you're talking about. But in a couple hours I'll be on my way to the closing in New Philadelphia, so whatever nonsense you're talking about needs to stop." He stepped around to the car door.

"Absolutely. We agree on that."

"I don't know what you're talking about," he repeated.

"I don't believe you."

He stared at her for a moment and then shook his head, yanked open his car door, and said, "I need to go."

And with that, he climbed into his car, put it in gear, and drove off. Cheryl was left standing in the parking lot silently, trying to make sense of it all. How could he? Didn't he care? What kind of...?

She tried to formulate words as his car pulled out of the lot and started down the street.

Now Cheryl was mad. She had been upset before and wanted to help Levi, but now she was just angry. She wanted to do anything she could to stop this man.

And yet...Cheryl thought for a minute and realized that she didn't know what more to do. She didn't have any more trails to search down.

But she couldn't just sit around and do nothing. It seemed their last hope really was finding that deed. How? If they hadn't found it by now...

Still, for lack of anything better to do, she decided the best thing she could do for the moment was to look for it. She knew Levi, Seth, and Emmon were supposed to be at Silas's house searching—and hopefully holding off Emmon's wife. Cheryl would head over there as well.

Cheryl drove down the hilly country roads faster than she normally would, but she seemed unable to stop herself from gunning it. They would need every minute to search.

Goodness. Now that so many people had pointed it out, Cheryl had to admit that the squeal coming from her hood really was bad. And it was getting louder. It was more like a shriek now. Well, after this week, she would get it checked out right away.

She pulled into the driveway and parked in front of the workshop door.

"Levi? Silas?" Cheryl called as she stepped inside the house.

"In here," Levi called. They were in the kitchen. Cheryl found Levi and Seth, along with Seth's brother Emmon, sitting around the wooden table, drinking from tall glasses. She knew that most of the extended family had traveled back to Michigan this morning, but Emmon and his wife had stayed behind for a few extra days to deal with wrapping up the legal and practical issues of his new house—and to clean it out. Cheryl was glad to see that at least they seemed to have held her off this morning.

"We could hear you coming," Seth said.

"Everyone in the county could hear you coming," Emmon said.

"What are you all doing in here?" Cheryl asked. Why weren't they searching for that deed?

"Strategizing," Seth said with the hint of a smile. He knew exactly what she'd been asking. "It has to be here somewhere. We are trying to think like my brother, trying to understand where he would have put it."

"We think it is possible it is misfiled in that office, but we do not have time to go through every file," Levi added.

Cheryl slowly lowered herself down into the last chair. "What have you come up with?"

Emmon gave a small, mirthless laugh. "The trouble is, no one really understood how my brother thinks."

"There must be a logic to it, we just cannot see what it is," Levi said.

Cheryl thought for a moment. "Did any of you ever actually see the deed?"

All three men shook their heads.

She decided not to go any farther down that road. It wouldn't help anything at this point.

Cheryl turned things around in her head, looking for anything that made sense.

"He must have been thinking about the land when he updated his will," Cheryl said. "It's possible he had the deed out then."

Emmon shrugged. "But when was that?"

Something niggled at the back of Cheryl's mind. Something to do with having the will drawn up. What had Luke Bradshaw told her? She thought for a moment.

"November." It had come out of nowhere, but suddenly she was sure she was right. Luke Bradshaw had mentioned that he'd updated the will then.

All three men were staring at her.

"That's what the lawyer told me. That Silas updated it in November."

Seth nodded. "I think you are probably right, actually. I believe it was around this time that he told me he was going to leave the land to Levi in his will."

"Okay. So it's feasible he might have had the deed out while he was thinking about the will," Cheryl said. The men looked dubious, but she continued. "We just need to figure out what else he had out on his desk around that time. Maybe it got misfiled with some of those papers."

"Even if that is true, how would we know which files to look in?" Seth asked, shaking his head. "You have seen that unusual filing system he had. We would not know where to start."

Cheryl thought about this and realized he was right. Even if she could figure out what other papers he'd been working on in November, and even if by some miracle he'd had the deed out and happened to have misfiled it with whatever else he was working on at the time, she would have no idea how to find it. And that was a lot of ifs.

Emmon's chair scraped across the floor as he pushed himself up. "I am going to search in his workshop one more time."

Seth nodded, his face sad. "I will check the barn."

Levi looked around the small tidy kitchen. "I guess I will see if it is stuck in some strange place in here."

So they were giving up on the files. Well, she could admit that it was unlikely they would find it, even if it was buried in there somewhere, but Cheryl wasn't ready to give up on her idea yet. There had to be a way to make sense of what other papers Silas had been dealing with in November. "I'll keep trying the files in the office," Cheryl said.

The men started to scatter, and so she pushed herself up and walked down the hall toward the office. She took in the simple desk, the small fireplace, the rows of filing cabinets. She looked again at the cross-stitched piece on the wall. *Beloved, let us love one another.*

Greta Yoder had said that what she was looking for was usually right out there in plain sight. Cheryl looked around the small room, searching. Looking for anything that might give her a clue as to what this Amish man had been thinking. What was in plain sight in this room?

Then she walked over to the wall and lifted the framed verse off the hook. This verse had been the key to opening the safe... Could it hold more secrets?

She turned the frame over and saw that the back was held on with yellowed tape. It was difficult to tell how long it had been in place. Carefully, Cheryl used her thumbnail to slice open the tape, and then slowly she lifted the back off the frame. Beneath the cardboard backing was a piece of heavy cardstock, the thick embroidery fabric wrapped around it, and a mat. She lifted the layers apart and searched through them, but there was nothing else.

Cheryl tried not to feel disappointed. It was silly to think that Silas would have sealed it up in the back of an embroidered decoration like this. But still, somehow, she couldn't help but feel a bit let down.

She turned then to the filing cabinets. Assuming her premise was right—that Silas had had the deed out when he was updating his will in November and had simply misfiled it with other paperwork that had been out at the same time—she just needed to know what he'd been working on in November.

There had to be some way to figure out what that was.

She dropped down into the office chair and tried to think. How would she know what projects Silas had been working on when?

Then she had an idea. It was probably silly. There was very little chance this would actually pan out... Still, she pulled her phone from her purse and pulled up the Web site Yelp, where people rated his business. This was the page she'd come across early on, when she was trying to find out information about Silas. Just as she remembered, most customers had given Silas a very high rating. And... there. Just as she remembered, the reviewers usually mentioned what sort of project he had been working on for them.

The most recent review, posted to the site just three weeks ago, said what a wonderful job Silas had done re-covering an armchair. The review before that referenced a set of kitchen chairs Silas had refinished. She scrolled back, looking for reviews posted in November.

There. One made mention of a table Silas had repaired. The name of the person who posted that review was named AMDavey. Was Davey a first name? A last name? Did *A* and *M* stand for names, or time of day, or something else altogether? There was no way to know. Cheryl moved to the cabinet where the files for tables were kept, and she opened up a drawer, looking through the *A*s, and then the *M*s, and then the *D*s—and then she found it. A file labeled Addison Marie Davey. Cheryl pulled the folder out, and sure enough, there were drawings of a table as well as extensive notes outlining what he had done to fix the table. There was also an invoice, stamped Paid.

It wasn't exactly what she'd been looking for, but it did show that there was some logic to these files after all. She scrolled down and looked at the next review. Someone named Deb Futter had posted a review about the excellent work Silas had done refinishing a coffee table she'd spilled nail polish remover on. *Let's see.* A coffee table was probably still in the table files, Cheryl thought. She went there and dug through the files until she located the file and checked the folder. Another drawing, more detailed notes, another stamped invoice. No deed.

Cheryl looked through the files for an ottoman and another armchair, and then the last review posted in November was a loveseat he'd upholstered.

Probably with the couches, Cheryl thought. She located the file without too much trouble and flipped through it quickly, seeing exactly what she expected: drawing, notes, invoice…but wait. What was this?

There was one more piece of paper tucked away at the back of the file. Cheryl pulled it out and looked at it.

Her eyes widened.

Could it be?

She stared at it. Forced herself to read it slowly.

And then, in the most un-Amish way possible, she shrieked, "I found it!"

Chapter Thirteen

In Cheryl's experience, Amish men didn't typically show much emotion. They tended to be calm, stoic, and guarded. Which was what made it even more extraordinary when Seth let out a whoop and tears sprang up in Levi's eyes. He tried to wipe them away before Cheryl saw them, so she pretended not to notice, but in truth her heart ached. She had never seen Levi so happy before.

Levi, Seth, Emmon, and Cheryl were all crowded into the small office at Silas's house, and they all looked at the paper, reading it over and over. Yes, this really was it. She was surprised to see how ordinary it looked, how there was a border around the edges, like it was a certificate of excellence from an elementary school. It was just the writing in the center that made it valuable, granting the land in question to Silas Ervin Miller. It was amazing how this one little piece of paper could make such a difference.

"How did you...?"

"Where was...?"

Cheryl waved away their questions. "I'll explain in just a minute. The first thing I need to do is call Luke Bradshaw."

Cheryl saw a look of distaste cross Seth's face, but she just smiled and grabbed her phone, which was still sitting on the desk. She pulled up his name and dialed.

"Come on, come on," she muttered as the line rang.

"Hello? Cheryl?"

"Luke. I got it."

"You got what?"

"The deed. We found it."

"The deed for the land?"

"Yes, the one we have been looking for this whole time."

"Oh my goodness." There was noise on his end of the phone—people talking, laughing, footsteps echoing. He must still be at the county office. "You're serious?"

"I am. This should be enough to stop the sale, right?"

"It should indeed. I'm still at the courthouse waiting to get in front of the judge, but you need to get here ASAP with that deed."

She checked the time on the small clock on the wall. They still had two hours until the closing was supposed to start. They would make it with time to spare.

"We're on our way."

She hung up and turned to the men. "We need to get to the courthouse right away."

For a moment no one moved, and she started to wonder if they had heard her, but then, as if at some silent cue, they all sprang into action. Seth grabbed the deed, and Levi and Emmon started toward the door.

A few minutes later, all three Amish men were strapped into her car and she was pulling out of the driveway on to the road. Cheryl was just about to start explaining how she had located the file when she heard something. It sounded like a loud pop, and it came from under the hood of her car.

"What was that?" Emmon, in the passenger seat, turned to Cheryl.

The air conditioner, which had been pumping out cool air on high speed, went dead.

"I don't know, but I'm sure it's fine..."

But even as she said the words, she knew it was not fine. Suddenly her steering wheel was very hard to control, and a red battery light had just appeared on her dashboard.

"I think you should pull over," Seth said, his voice calm but authoritative.

"I'm sure it's okay. It's just something to do with the battery, but the car still drives, and we need to get to..."

"I do not think this is safe," Seth continued.

"Look at that." Levi was leaning forward from the backseat and pointing at some gauge on the dashboard. "I do not think that is supposed to be doing that."

Cheryl slowed down and looked at the temperature gauge. It had a little needle that was going up against a colored background, from green to yellow to red. She watched as the needle moved solidly into the red zone. She may not know very much about cars, but she was pretty sure this was a bad sign. Reluctantly, she slowed the car down and pulled over to the side of the road. For a moment, no one said anything. They all looked at each other, trying to figure out what to do. Cheryl obviously couldn't drive them to the courthouse now.

"I could call someone to come and get us." Cheryl tried to think of who though. Kathy Snyder was her first thought, but Kathy was out of town. And most other people she knew were working in their shops. But surely in a situation like this, they would come and help her...Jessica Stockton would do it! She pulled out her cell phone and dialed Jessica's number, but it rang and rang and then went to voice mail.

"We will take the buggy," Levi said.

"All the way to New Philadelphia?" Cheryl asked. "Will it go that far?" New Philadelphia was only about thirteen miles from Sugarcreek, but she knew the Amish didn't like to take their buggies much more than ten miles if they could avoid it.

"We are on the right side of town at least." Seth was right, Cheryl realized. They were already a couple miles out of town in the right direction.

"But..." How fast did buggies travel? To Cheryl, who passed them regularly, buggies seemed to drive painfully slowly. "Will we be able to make it in time?"

Seth checked the clock on the dashboard. "We will if we hurry," he said. And just like that, the Amish men hopped out of the car and were running back toward the house. By the time Cheryl had called Luke Bradshaw to tell him it would take longer than she'd hoped to get there and then locked up the car and hurried back to the driveway, Levi was hitching up Sugar. Seth held out his hand to Cheryl, and she took it and he helped her step into the buggy. Cheryl settled on the hard second bench while Levi helped his father and uncle up and then sat down on the bench beside her.

Seth took the reins and said something to Sugar, and they started to move.

The metal wheels crunched against the dirt driveway, kicking up tiny stones and a cloud of dust, and Sugar's feet pounded against the hard dirt. Cheryl tried to settle back and enjoy the swaying rhythm of the ride, the feeling of Levi on the bench beside her, the relief that they had finally found the proof they needed...Cheryl leaned forward and looked around.

Oh my goodness. They were not even to the end of the driveway?!

"Does this thing go any faster?" she asked.

"No." Seth's simple, clear answer was unequivocal. There would be no arguing with how he drove his buggy.

Cheryl tried not to let impatience flare up. It was her fault after all that they had to take a buggy to New Philadelphia, but still, there had to be a faster way than this.

"We will make it," Emmon added.

Cheryl wasn't sure. She checked the time on her phone. 1:15. They still had an hour and forty-five minutes until the closing started, but at this pace, would they ever get there?

Hot air brushed past them. Cheryl missed her air-conditioning.

"So," Levi said, as they finally—finally—turned out on to the main road, "we have some time to kill. Will you tell us now how you found the deed?"

Cheryl smiled at him, grateful that he was trying to make it better, and then she told them how she had thought to look at the online reviews and used that to trace which projects he'd been working on at the same time as the deed. She had to explain to Emmon what Yelp was and how online reviews worked, and she pulled out her phone to show them. Emmon wondered if it worked in other places and asked her to look up his own furniture business in Michigan. He was delighted to see that it had many positive reviews. Then she looked up the Miller Maze and Petting Zoo, which had also been reviewed favorably. Cheryl almost choked when she saw that one review made reference to a "smokin' hot blond Amish guy" who worked there. Levi. Well, of course other people had noticed him. It was hard not to. Then conversation turned back to the search for the deed.

"So he simply misfiled it in the end," Levi said.

"He did. And that shouldn't have been a problem, since the county is supposed to have records of property sales, but in this case, they had been destroyed by the clerk." Cheryl then told them all about how she'd discovered who had been behind the missing files—leaving out any reference to Ruthanna so she didn't get in trouble—and about her recent conversation with Michael Borland.

Cheryl recounted as many details of the search over the past few days as she could, and then she looked out of the buggy to see where they were. Oh goodness. They were barely a mile down the road. This was going to take forever.

Levi turned his head and caught her eye. "We will make it," he said, and then he scooted over so his leg was almost touching hers. Cheryl could feel the heat of him through their clothes. Well, that was distracting, but not distracting enough to keep her mind off the fact that they were making a journey that should have taken twenty minutes in a car last nearly two hours.

"It is the Amish version of a high-speed chase," Levi joked, flashing her a crooked smile. Her heartbeat sped up, and she laughed, a genuine, heartfelt laugh.

Seth and Emmon began chatting quietly on the front bench, and for a minute Cheryl let her mind wander, thinking through the craziness of the past few days and about the mess at the Honey Bee, but finally her mind returned to the conversation with Aunt Mitzi last night. Levi seemed to understand what she was feeling and knew how to make her laugh, even when the last thing she felt like doing was laughing.

"Thank you for your help finding the deed," Levi said quietly.

"Of course. I wanted to help." She smiled. "I want you to have the land your uncle left you."

He looked at her, and for a moment his gaze was so intense she almost had to look away, but she couldn't bring herself to. "I want that too," he said.

"Will you move on to the land right away?" Cheryl asked. She couldn't imagine how disappointing it would be to visit Naomi and not see Levi there. But then, he was an Amish man in this thirties, and he couldn't live at home forever.

"Not right away," Levi said. "I will need to build a house, of course. And my father still appreciates the help with the farm and the petting zoo." He looked out the side of the buggy, away from Cheryl, but he leaned in almost imperceptibly. "The land is more for the future."

He didn't say any more, and Cheryl didn't want to press it, especially with his father and uncle in the front seat. But Cheryl wondered what the future looked like, in his mind. Was there a place for her in it?

"What will you grow on your land?" Cheryl asked. It seemed like a nice, safe question.

"Oh, many things," Levi said. "Corn and wheat, to be sure. Maybe alfalfa. I'd like to try my hand at soy too." He was quiet for a minute. "I will have a barn, of course, and keep horses and a few cows. Maybe some goats. I have always loved goat cheese."

Cheryl loved goat cheese too, from the basic chèvre to aged cheese with fancier rinds. She imagined making cheese fresh from milk produced right on her own land.

"I want to have a small garden near the house and grow vegetables and herbs."

Cheryl could almost picture it. A small fenced garden behind the big white house. A large barn sheltering the animals. Rows and rows of crops, reaching slowly and steadily up toward the heavens. Long winters, sheltered snugly inside the cozy house. Joyful harvests. Children running barefoot in the yard.

"It sounds like heaven," Cheryl said.

Levi didn't answer her for a moment, and then, slowly, he nodded. "It does, doesn't it?"

He shifted over a bit more, so his leg was pressed against hers. They rode like that, quietly imagining the future, for a good long while, and then Seth asked Cheryl to look up directions for the fastest way to the courthouse, and she realized they had reached the outskirts of New Philadelphia.

Cheryl checked the time. They were cutting it close. She used her phone to navigate the streets, and soon they were pulling into the parking lot.

They were greeted by a crowd of protesters, holding signs printed with slogans like Jail Fail! and No Jail in My Backyard! There were roughly two dozen people clapping and chanting, and several of them eyed the buggy as Seth guided Sugar to a parking area with hitching posts under a grove of trees. The time on Cheryl's phone read 3:09.

Seth tied Sugar to a light pole in the shade of a big leafy elm tree, gave her a pat on the nose, and promised her a snack as soon as they returned, and then they all ran for the door.

Halfway to the door, someone in the crowd yelled, "Hey, it's the girl from the article!"

Cheryl's spiky red hair was memorable enough that someone had recognized her from the photo in the paper.

"Are these the farmers they're trying to rip off?" someone else added, looking at the men with her.

"Yes," Cheryl called as she kept moving quickly toward the door. "And we have the deed!"

A cry went up, people cheering and clapping, and Cheryl felt tears spring to her eyes as they stepped through the glass front door. It wasn't just Levi who was affected by this after all. Everyone in the area was being saved from the installation of a jail.

Where are you? Cheryl texted to Luke Bradshaw.

Moments later he texted back, *Third floor, turn right and go down to the end of the hall.*

Cheryl directed them toward the bank of elevators, and then, as she pushed the button, Luke added, *Hurry.*

The elevators were agonizingly slow, but finally they stepped out into a long hallway. She followed Luke's directions, and a minute later she saw him standing outside a door at the end of the hall. He wore a sharp gray suit and clutched a leather briefcase under his arm.

"Let me see it," he said, and Levi handed over the deed. Luke looked at the paper, and then a slow smile spread across his face. "You really found it."

"Where is the closing?"

"They're in there." He jerked his thumb at the door. "The developer, his lawyer, and representatives from the county. They know I'm out here but insisted I stay outside since I didn't have proof." He grinned at Cheryl and then at Levi, Seth, and Emmon.

"You really rode all the way here in a buggy?"

"Yes," Cheryl said. "It was quite an experience."

"Some of us do not mind riding in buggies," Seth said. "We do it all the time." For a moment she thought he was upset, but then she realized that he was actually making a joke.

Cheryl laughed, a too-loud laugh that echoed down the hallway, letting out the anxiety and relief she felt.

Luke chuckled too and then, with a serious look on his face, asked, "Are you ready to get your land back?"

Cheryl grinned, and the Amish men nodded, and then Luke pushed the door open.

Behind the door was a conference room, and five men were gathered around a long table. Piles of papers were strewn across the table, and Michael was in the process of signing some document. They all looked up when the door opened. Michael looked stricken, while most of the rest of the men simply seemed confused to see Luke Bradshaw walk in followed by Cheryl and three Amish men.

"I have proof that that parcel of land you are attempting to sell actually belonged to Silas Miller and now should pass to his heir Levi Miller," he said and slid the deed down in front of the men from the county.

The men looked up, looked at each other, and then looked down at the paper.

"Is this for real?" a balding, bespectacled man in a three-piece suit said.

"It is very much for real. It is exactly what I warned you I would present."

"But there is no record of it in the county's files," Michael said. He looked at Cheryl and then at the Amish men, and he looked . . . well, Cheryl was surprised to see that he looked confused more than anything.

"That very convenient fact was made possible by your own sister," Luke Bradshaw said. A look Cheryl couldn't read passed over Michael's face. "As you well know."

"Perhaps your clients can wait outside while we discuss this?" one of the men in suits said to Luke, looking at the Amish men and Cheryl. He didn't want them here while they worked out who was stealing and how. Cheryl felt her anger flare up. What, the shady developer could stay here with his lawyer while the woman and the Amish men were being kicked out? Cheryl wasn't going to stand for that kind of sexist, bigoted behavior.

"No way," Cheryl said. "These men own this land. You can't just kick them out while you…"

"Cheryl, maybe it is for the best," Seth said quietly.

She turned and looked at him and then at the other Amish men, who nodded as well.

"You really want to just let *him* handle this?" she said, jerking her thumb at the lawyer they had told her they didn't trust. She was pretty sure he would be competent, but Seth had said he didn't believe him.

"No," Seth said. "We have done our best. Now we will let Gott handle it."

With that, all of Cheryl's anger and frustration melted away. She couldn't argue with that logic. She trusted that Luke would do his best to prove that the land was now Levi's.

"We will wait outside," Emmon said to Luke, and they started out. Cheryl had no choice but to follow them.

After she stepped into the hallway, the door closed behind them, and they were alone in the long, silent hallway. Seth and Emmon started talking in Pennsylvania Dutch, and Levi smiled at Cheryl but didn't seem to know what to say. Cheryl wanted more than anything to go over and wrap her arms around him, to tell him it was all going to be okay now, but she couldn't. Would she ever be able to?

To distract herself, Cheryl started pacing up and down the long hallway. After her first trip up and back, Levi started walking next to her. Silently, they walked together, up and back, up and back, their steps in rhythm.

And then, after what felt like hours, but according to her phone had only been ten minutes, Luke Bradshaw stepped back out into the hallway.

"It's done," he said. "The sale is void. The land belongs to Levi. There will be no jail."

Cheryl let out a whoop, and even Seth and Emmon shouted with joy. Levi was quiet and almost looked like he might faint, but Cheryl could see in his face that a burden had been lifted.

"Well, technically, it's still wrapped up in probate, and we'll need to file the paperwork to get the land transferred to Levi, but it will be yours soon," Luke clarified.

"That is good enough for me." Levi finally smiled.

"Come with me, and I'll explain everything," Luke said. He led them down the hallway and down the elevators back to the lobby. They moved to the side of the large airy lobby, out of the way, but still inside the air-conditioning, and Seth started to ask questions about the next steps in the probate process. Emmon was very interested in hearing about that as well. Cheryl knew that mattered to these men, but all she wanted to know about was what had happened inside that room. Still, she couldn't interrupt.

Maybe once they'd gotten all the legal stuff out of the way, Luke would be able to tell them...

But then Cheryl was startled to see Michael Borland and his lawyer step out of the elevators. She supposed he had no business here anymore and was on his way out. Cheryl looked at him and then at the men she was with. Luke was still droning on about probate court. Before she could second-guess herself, Cheryl stepped away from the Amish men and crossed the lobby, meeting Michael squarely in the center of the room.

"I hope you'll think about this meeting next time you try to steal land from someone," she said. "Just because they're Amish, it doesn't mean they're stupid and you can take advantage of them, and I hope you..."

"Wait." He held up his hands. "Just wait. That's not fair."

"They have every legal right to this land, and just because you have all this money behind you, it doesn't mean..."

"I didn't know." The men walking with him stopped, but Michael waved for them to keep going, so they moved toward the doors, and it was just Cheryl and the developer standing in the center of the room.

"You can't just go around trying to steal people's land."

"I didn't know my sister had taken the records." He adjusted the strap of the leather messenger bag he had strung around his shoulders.

"And I'm the Queen of England. I hope you..."

"No, listen to me. Please, just listen." He shoved his hands into his pockets, and a class ring caught on the fabric.

Cheryl crossed her arms over her chest. "I'm listening. This should be good."

"I wasn't trying to steal anything, I promise. And it wasn't until your lawyer just told me about the missing electronic records and that my sister was involved that I realized what was going on."

"I told you about it earlier today."

He shrugged. "I thought you were some crazy person making things up." He gave her a sheepish smile. "Sorry. But you were kind of stalking me, waiting by my car."

Okay, she had to admit she could sort of see his point there. Still, that didn't let him off the hook. Cheryl stared him down. "You just happened to try to buy the land that by coincidence your sister had destroyed the records for?"

He shook his head. "I once dated a girl who worked for the man who lived there. An Amish girl."

"Ruthanna."

"You know her?"

Cheryl nodded. "It was Ruthanna who discovered that the county's electronic records for the land had been deleted by your sister."

"She discovered that?" He nodded, a proud look on his face. "I thought she didn't use computers anymore."

"She has friends," Cheryl said, and he laughed. It echoed off the high ceilings and attracted the attention of the security guard in the corner, who was eyeing them.

"You have to admit it looks pretty suspicious," Cheryl said. "Your dating the girl who worked there and then mysteriously having all impediments to your buying it disappear."

"I guess it may look that way, but you have to believe me. It was because of Ruthanna that I first saw the land. I came to pick her up from work one time and noticed what a large farm it was, and she told me there were two plots of land. I asked my sister to look into it for me, and she told me it was owned by the county. I had no reason to doubt her."

"But if she pointed it out several years ago and you thought he didn't own the land, why didn't you try to buy it then? Why wait until he died?"

"I offered to buy it from him, many times. But he wouldn't sell. I gave him my card in case he ever wanted to sell, and he did not."

"But if he didn't own the land, how were you planning to buy it from him?"

"I figured we would figure it out."

This sounded sketchy to Cheryl, but she didn't know what to say.

"If you knew, or thought you knew, that the land was technically marked as owned by the county, why didn't you try to just buy it out from under him years ago?"

"Ruthanna asked me not to." He shrugged.

Cheryl waited for him to go on, but that seemed to be his whole explanation.

"You were looking at a real estate deal that probably could have made you millions, but you didn't move on it because an Amish girl asked you not to?"

"When you put it like that, it sounds unlikely," he admitted. "But she wasn't just some Amish girl. I loved her. It didn't work out, obviously, but back then I really thought we might have a future together. So I promised her I wouldn't take the land from Silas and I wouldn't try to buy it until he died."

"And then, once he died, you didn't waste any time."

"As you mentioned, it would have been a very lucrative development deal." He shrugged. "But please believe me, I was under the impression that the land was owned by the county. I did not realize my sister had made the records disappear."

"Has she 'made records disappear' in the past? This isn't the first time your developments have come under question."

"I don't know. I hope not."

"I'm sure the county will be very interested to hear about that."

"I'm sure they will. And hey, if what you're saying is true, then she should be punished." He didn't say anything for a moment, and then he sighed and shook his head. "My sister has always been...Well, she's always had a wild streak. She's gotten in trouble with the law a few times. We thought she'd finally settled down, but I guess that was too much to hope for."

Cheryl could see that he really did care about his sister, and now that her anger had cooled and she'd had a few minutes to calm down, she was starting to feel almost a bit sorry for this guy. Just a bit. Not enough to actually let him off the hook.

"She was trying to help me out, I guess, and probably thought she would get some kind of kickback." He looked chagrined. "I've given her some nice thank-you gifts for pointing me toward available land in the past. It was all very informal, just that she'd spot something that was up for sale and point it out to me, and I'd take her out for a nice dinner and buy her something nice as a thank-you."

That sounded a bit shady to Cheryl, but she let him continue. "Well, if this had gone through, this would have been the biggest deal in my career, and I think she was thinking there might be more than a dinner and some jewelry in it for her."

"Would there have been?"

He shrugged. "Maybe. I don't know. It doesn't matter now anyway."

Cheryl eyed him, trying to figure out whether she could believe him.

"But when I tried to tell you, you ignored my messages and wouldn't see me."

"I didn't know who you were or what you were talking about. I get hundreds of messages a day," he said. "I did not ignore you because I didn't want to know the truth about this land. I ignored you because if I stopped to listen to everyone who contacted me every day, I would never get anything done."

Cheryl eyed him. He could be telling more tales, but it did seem that he'd been misled and was not the lying, cheating land thief she'd built him up to be in her head.

"The point is, I did not mean to try to steal that land."

"Okay..." Cheryl wasn't sure what more to say. Despite his assurances to the contrary, it sure did look suspicious.

"And I'm sorry for the trouble I've caused."

Cheryl nodded.

"If it's okay, I'd like to say as much to those gentlemen over there," he said, nodding to Seth, Levi, and Emmon. The Amish men were standing shoulder to shoulder, watching this exchange, though they were too far away to hear what was being said.

"You're going to apologize to them?" Cheryl asked. This should be good. He acted like saying he was sorry would be enough to make them all forget he'd nearly stolen Levi's inheritance.

Michael nodded, and then he turned and started across the floor. Cheryl followed a few steps behind and stopped a bit behind him, watching as he apologized and then held out a hand to each man. The Amish men took his hand in turn and nodded as he explained to them what he had just told her. And then, one by one, the Amish men bowed their heads and told him they forgave him.

At first Cheryl couldn't believe what she was seeing. They just forgave him? Just like that? But then after she'd had a moment to process the scene, she realized she should have expected it. This was what the Amish did. Forgiveness was part of their way of life.

Cheryl realized as she stood here that it needed to be part of hers as well. Whether or not Michael really had meant to take that land away, he had apologized for it. And as much as everything in her revolted against the idea, she realized she needed to follow the lead of her Amish friends.

When Michael finally turned away, she saw that he had tears in his eyes. Cheryl hadn't expected that. She felt her own tears sting her eyes, and she tried to push them back. Michael thanked the Amish men and then waved and nodded at Cheryl as he walked toward the door.

"Wait," Cheryl called. She hurried over to his side. "I'm sorry I judged you wrongly."

"Thank you," Michael said. He nodded, and then he turned toward the door. They all watched as the developer joined up with his lawyer and stepped out of the glass doors. The gathered crowd booed as he walked past.

Cheryl did not want to come to his rescue. The last thing she wanted to do right now was publicly defend him. But she knew she had to. Cheryl grasped the heavy glass door, stepped outside, and caught the attention of the crowd.

"The sale was blocked. The jail will not be built," she said.

The resulting shouts and cheers provided enough of a distraction that Michael was able to slip away. Good. She didn't want to run into him again, but she had to admit that it hadn't been entirely his fault.

Cheryl was approached by a woman who introduced herself as Nancy Chandler, and Cheryl recognized her voice right away. This was the reporter she'd spoken to earlier in the week. Nancy asked if she could answer a few questions. She also wanted to talk to the Amish men, but they declined, preferring to use the time to deal with their horse. But Seth encouraged Cheryl to speak for them.

Finally, the small crowd cleared out, and Cheryl wasn't sure what to do. A thousand feelings—elation, humility, embarrassment, love—all flooded through her. She feared that if she opened her mouth, she'd start crying.

Finally, Seth came over and stood in front of her.

"We had better get going," he said, his voice thick. "We have a long ride home."

Cheryl laughed. She had forgotten that they would need to take a buggy ride back to Sugarcreek.

As soon as they were all settled into the buggy and had started off down the road, back toward Sugarcreek, Levi turned to Cheryl.

"I hope you never get mad at me like you got mad at that man," he said.

Cheryl laughed. It felt good to laugh.

"I can't imagine I ever would."

Levi shrugged. "I do not know. When two people spend much time together, are they not certain to disagree sometimes?"

Cheryl thought back through what he'd just said. He was planning on spending a lot of time with her, he'd said. What did that mean? Was he saying he was imagining what a life with her might look like? Was he thinking about the future of the land he was now to inherit? Or was Cheryl reading too much into an innocent question?

"I just hope you will go easy on me." He gave her a crooked smile, and her stomach warmed.

"How about this: you don't try to take my inheritance, and I won't rip into you," Cheryl said.

"It is a deal." Levi grinned.

Cheryl didn't know what would happen with his land or whether she would have a part in his future or not, but one thing she did know was that she was grateful to have this man in her life. Only God knew what the future held, but right now Cheryl would just enjoy the blessing of being near him.

CHAPTER FOURTEEN

A s Cheryl stood by the side of the road next to her disabled car waiting for the tow truck to show up, her phone rang. She was delighted to see that Kathy Snyder was calling.

"Kathy! How's your mother doing?"

Levi and Seth had dropped her off here at her insistence. They had wanted to wait for the tow truck with her, but she knew that they still had chores waiting for them and that Naomi would be worried, so she shooed them off and had called the roadside assistance company. It was getting on toward evening, and now that the sun was hanging lower in the sky, a nice breeze had picked up, rustling the corn stalks behind her along this stretch of country road.

"Much better. In fact, she's doing so well that we were starting to drive each other crazy, and I'm on my way back to Sugarcreek. I was planning to head straight to the Honey Bee. Want to meet me there? I brought you something to thank you for all you did."

"You're coming back early?" Cheryl's heart dropped into her stomach. She'd been planning on having tomorrow to, well, clean things up a bit before Kathy saw the state of her café.

"Yep. I'm on my way now. I should be there right around six. Does that work for you?"

"Six?" Cheryl looked at her watch. The tow truck was supposed to be here in the next five minutes, and they would bring a rental car that Cheryl could use until her own car was repaired. She could make it by six. And as much as she was dreading facing Kathy and telling her everything that had gone wrong at the café, Cheryl knew that delaying the inevitable would only make it worse.

"Sure. I'll see you there at six," she said.

A few minutes later her car was loaded up onto the tow truck and she was behind the wheel of a sporty new rental, heading back down the country roads toward town.

When she pulled up in front of the Honey Bee, Kathy's car was already parked in the small lot. Oh dear. Cheryl had hoped to get there before Kathy, to have a little time to explain before she saw the mess that was left of her café.

Cheryl climbed the steps of the front porch and opened the front door.

"Hi there," Kathy said, a little too brightly, Cheryl thought. She was behind the counter sweeping the floor. No one was this happy sweeping a floor. Was she masking how upset she was?

"Hi, Kathy." Cheryl stepped in tentatively.

Kathy pointed at a box of high-end chocolates sitting on one of the tables. "That's for you. It's not enough to thank you for all you've done, but I wanted to get you something."

"Thank you." Cheryl felt her cheeks flush. "It's really not necessary. Believe me."

"Oh, nonsense." Kathy moved the broom across the floor. "How were things here?"

How were things here? Cheryl tried to figure out how to answer that. How much did Kathy know? She decided to deflect the question.

"How are you? How did it go with your mom?" She closed the door behind her and looked around. Deborah Hoffman had done a pretty good job of cleaning up in here this afternoon, but the trash bins were still overflowing, there was milk spilled all over the condiment station, and the sandwich case had sandwiches piled up every which way.

"It was really great to be there with her," Kathy said. "I was glad to be able to help her after all she's done for me. And I cannot thank you enough for all you did to keep this place running while I was gone."

Cheryl hesitated. There didn't seem to be any malice in her voice, but she couldn't be serious, right?

"What's wrong?" Kathy stopped sweeping and looked around.

"I'm just..." Cheryl didn't know what to say. "I'm so sorry for the way things look in here, and for how it all went."

"What do you mean? You're sorry for organizing a volunteer army to keep my shop open for me? I hardly think you need to apologize for that."

Oh dear. She didn't know the depth of the trouble then.

"Well, it didn't go exactly flawlessly. I fear some of your regulars may have been frustrated by how long things took sometimes." That was putting it mildly.

"They'll get over it."

"A few of the volunteers didn't really know how to make espresso drinks."

"So people got to branch out and try new things. Good."

Cheryl tried again. "Sometimes trash didn't get taken out or milk didn't get refilled."

"I'm not worried."

"There was a bit of an issue with the plumbing."

Kathy shrugged. "If you're trying to convince me I shouldn't be grateful for your help, it's not going to work."

"It's not that." Cheryl tried to think of how to say this. "But I know we weren't able to run the café the way you run it, and I worry we let you down. I can't help but wonder if it might have been better for your business if you'd simply closed this week."

Kathy rested the broom against the counter and leaned back against the sink. "You're sweet, but I know for a fact you're wrong. It would not have been better if I'd simply closed. Sure, maybe I'll have to give away a few sandwiches and drinks to gain back a customer or two, but that's not a big deal. What is a big deal is that I was able to see how much my friends were willing to sacrifice to help me out, and I will never be able to convey how much that means to me."

Cheryl didn't know what to say. She appreciated Kathy's words, but she still wasn't sure Kathy understood how badly they'd messed things up for her.

"When I first moved to Sugarcreek, I didn't know anyone," Kathy said. "I was just intrigued by the area and wanted a slower pace of life. But in the time I've been here, you guys—you and Greta, Marion, Gail, and the others who helped me this week—have become my family. And you showed me that this week. I will always be thankful for what you've done, not just this week, to make me feel at home in Sugarcreek." She crossed her arms over her chest. "So I don't care at all that things didn't go perfectly. I don't care if I have a plumber's bill to pay or that I need to make nice with the bread delivery man. None of that matters. Your willingness to help means so much to me, and I can't ever thank you enough."

Cheryl didn't know what to say. She felt tears prick at her eyes.

"Your business may never be the same."

"And neither will my heart."

Kathy gave her a genuine smile, and she reached for a basket of napkins as tears spilled out of Cheryl's eyes. She handed them to her friend silently. Cheryl used one to dab at her face.

"Would you like anything to eat?" Kathy said, indicating the sandwich case. "They're going in the trash otherwise."

Cheryl tossed the tissue into the overflowing trash bin. She glanced at the sandwich case, and her stomach growled. She realized she hadn't eaten anything since breakfast. "Actually, that would be amazing," she said.

"What about coffee?" Kathy nodded at the espresso maker. "I could make you a latte. You know, just so you don't forget what a real drink tastes like."

Ooh. Suddenly a real espresso drink, with steamed milk and rich dark coffee, made by someone who knew what they were doing, sounded amazing. "Decaf?"

"Coming right up."

Kathy turned and started pulling the espresso.

"So what all did I miss this week? Anything exciting happen in Sugarcreek while I was gone?" She poured milk into a jug and lowered the arm and then turned on the machine, steaming the milk.

Cheryl laughed. She realized Kathy didn't know anything about the search for the deed that had kept Cheryl busy this week, or how close Levi had almost come to losing everything.

"Oh, you know, just your average week in Sugarcreek," she said with a laugh.

"Sounds like there's a story there." Kathy poured the milk into the cup, making a perfect leaf design with the foam, and then handed it over to Cheryl. "How about if I grab a drink too and you can tell me all about it?"

Cheryl felt dead on her feet, and there was still so much to clean up in here. And after that, she should probably go back to the Swiss Miss and make sure everything was closed and locked up properly for the night. There were many things she needed to do, but suddenly there was nothing she wanted more than to sit and catch up with her friend.

"That would be perfect," Cheryl said.

There would always be more to do. Things to clean and businesses to run. But if this week had taught her anything, it was that these relationships—these people God had placed in her life—really mattered. Cleaning could wait. Cheryl didn't know how many days were left ahead of her. No one could know when God might call them home. Cheryl wanted to make sure she was using every one of her days well. Right now spending time enjoying the friend God had brought into her life sounded like the best thing she could do on this summer evening.

"But only if we can sit on the porch."

"I like the way you think."

Kathy grabbed a sandwich for Cheryl and took their coffees, and together they stepped out on to the wooden porch. The sun was falling lower in the sky, casting a golden glow over the charming little town of Sugarcreek. The air had cooled, and the breeze carried the scent of fresh country air and roses from the pots on the railing. Cheryl sighed as she sank into a comfortable Adirondack chair.

She didn't know how Levi's new land would change things or if she and Levi could ever create a life together. She didn't know when Aunt Mitzi might come back from Papua New Guinea or how things would change if she did. She had no idea how long she'd get to live in Sugarcreek.

Cheryl thought about Silas, about the Amish community that had loved him, and how they were starting to feel more and more like her family too.

She took a sip of her coffee and waved at Jacob Hoffman, who was hitching up his horse to head home for the day.

Cheryl didn't know what the future held, but she did know this: God brought her to Sugarcreek, and He had a plan for her future.

Looking out at the community she had come to call home, Cheryl couldn't wait to see what more God had in store.

Author Letter

Dear Reader,

One of my favorite things about writing for this series is learning how the Amish—a totally different culture from ours—think about the world. I love learning about why they do things the way they do, and I am constantly surprised and challenged to question why I believe what I do.

I can't do my job without my computer or my phone, but the more I read about why the Amish avoid bringing these devices into their homes—they are allowed to use them at their jobs if needed—the more I love the idea of avoiding them when my husband or kids are around. The less time I spend distracted by the outside world, the more value I find in enjoying the people around me.

The more I read about the intentional choices the Amish make about parenting—eating meals together, requiring young children to do chores, prioritizing time together as a family—the more Amish my own parenting seems to become.

When I first heard that many Amish have wills, I found the idea delightfully funny. But then I realized, *Why not?* The Amish need to protect and pass on their assets just like everyone else.

That was the launching place for this story. The more I dug into it, the more I realized that a will is just a legal document for allocating resources. Their culture has its own traditions, such as the fact that the youngest son inherits the family farm. I'm a long way from having assets to pass down—I'm still trying to pay for nursery school!—but hearing about these different traditions challenged me to think about why we do things the way we do and to wonder if there's a better way.

I hope the surprises I find as I learn more about these fascinating and inspiring people will continue to challenge my thinking, and I hope you enjoy reading this book as much as I enjoyed writing it!

Best,

Elizabeth Adams

About the Author

Elizabeth Adams lives in New York City with her husband and two young daughters. When she's not writing, she spends time cleaning up after two devious cats and trying to find time to read mysteries.

Fun Fact about
the Amish or Sugarcreek, Ohio

Death is never a fun subject. But Silas Miller is fictional, so I will admit that I did enjoy learning more about how the Amish think about death and value life as I worked on this story.

I loved learning about the way the community comes together to help the grieving family prepare for the funeral by cooking, cleaning, taking over farm chores, and by helping prepare for visiting relatives. I was fascinated by how the Amish men come together to dig the grave by hand—what else would they do, after all?—and how the Amish have their own cemeteries. I loved the images I saw of long lines of buggies, one after another after another, heading to the grave site. Something about that picture symbolized how the members of these communities support one another. I also really loved the fact that most Amish communities don't eulogize the dead at their funerals, but focus their funeral service on praising the Giver of Life.

Of course, death is difficult in any culture, but I really appreciated reading about how the Amish understand that death is a part of life. It's hard to think about it like that, but I appreciate how it reminds me to really focus on trying to serve God and each other with every day of life I am given.

Something Delicious from Our Sugarcreek Friends

Kathy Snyder's Chocolate Chip Scones
(This is the recipe Cheryl couldn't find!)

2 cups all-purpose flour

⅓ cup sugar

1 teaspoon baking powder

½ teaspoon baking soda

½ teaspoon salt

6 tablespoons unsalted butter, chilled and diced

¾ cup miniature semisweet chocolate chips

¾ cup buttermilk

1 large egg yolk

1 teaspoon vanilla extract

Whipped cream

Grease baking sheet and preheat oven to four hundred degrees. Stir together the flour, sugar, baking powder, baking soda, and salt. Add butter and mix together with your fingers until it's the size of rice. Stir in chocolate chips. In a separate bowl, mix together buttermilk, egg yolk, and vanilla. Add to dry ingredients and mix together until the flour mixture is moist. Try not to overmix. Gather dough into a ball and press it out on a floured cutting board until it's about eight inches around. Cut it into six wedges. Pull wedges apart and place on prepared baking sheet. Bake until scones are crusty on top and toothpick inserted into the center comes out clean. This will take about twenty minutes. Best served warm, topped with fresh whipped cream.

Read on for a sneak peek of another exciting book
in the series Sugarcreek Amish Mysteries!

Shoo, Fly, Shoo!
by Amy Lillard

Sirens blaring, lights twirling, Sugarcreek's finest raced past the
Miller farm.

"That looks like trouble." Cheryl Cooper turned to her friend
as the sirens wailed by.

"Oh, this can't be good." A frown creased Naomi Miller's brow.
"The Albert Yoders live down there."

Cheryl had heard of the family. Albert Yoder was a successful
dairy farmer, producing what some considered the finest milk in
the community. "You think there's trouble at the Yoder farm?"

Naomi continued to stare off into the distance, her gaze fixed
in the direction where the police cars disappeared. "Rebekah Yoder
is going to have a baby. This time has not been easy for her."

Cheryl followed Naomi's gaze but shook her head. "Why
would Rebekah need a police car if she's gone into labor?"

"I do not know."

But Cheryl did. This was trouble of a different sort.

"I need to go down there." Naomi whirled on her heel and
headed back into the house.

Cheryl had come out to the Miller farm for a quick afternoon visit and to see a new animal for their petting zoo, a black alpaca with long eyelashes and a sweet face. Naomi had been asking her for days to come out and see the creature, but Cheryl had to put her off. Summertime in Sugarcreek meant more tourists than locals, and the Swiss Miss had been busier than ever.

"You mean now?" she asked as Naomi rushed from the house and whistled for her horse. "It would be so much quicker in my car."

Naomi gave her buggy horse a pat on the neck and then turned back to Cheryl. "Thank you, Cheryl Cooper."

The pair hopped into the car, and Cheryl headed in the direction where the police cars had disappeared. She couldn't imagine what police cars had to do with a pregnant woman, and she wasn't sure she wanted to know. She cast a quick look at Naomi. Her friend sat ramrod straight in the passenger side, hands folded primly in her lap, eyes trained firmly ahead. She wasn't sure either one of them was prepared for what could be waiting at the Yoder farm. She could only pray that it was nothing as grisly as prime-time television portrayed.

A few minutes later, Cheryl pulled her little blue sedan into utter chaos. She cut the engine as Naomi got out of the car and rushed into the fray, undoubtedly looking for Rebekah Yoder.

Cheryl paused for a moment just to take it all in. Aside from the two police cars, there was a fire truck, a bulldozer, and a backhoe. The police officers were talking to different people. Chief Twitchell was taking notes on his little memo book as an older

Amish man spoke. His beard was completely gray, though his eyes flashed blue fire behind his wire-rimmed glasses. He gestured wildly with his hands as Twitchell nodded and continued to write.

Cheryl watched, entranced. She had never seen anyone Amish use such animated gestures before. He was all but shouting as he nodded and pointed. Whatever had happened, it seemed like a pretty big deal. But if the police were talking to the farm owner, Cheryl could only assume that the older man was none other than Albert Yoder. If that was the case, then hopefully everything was okay with Rebekah.

She allowed her gaze to run over the crowd of people. Aside from the chief, there were two policemen, four or five men in hard hats, a handful of firemen, a bevy of children, and at least a dozen gawkers. No doubt police sirens brought out the Amish and English alike.

She spotted Naomi in the bustle of people. Her friend wound through the crowd until she reached an Amish woman about the same age as she, though of opposite build. The woman wore a green dress and a black day apron, and she seemed as round as Naomi was thin. Cheryl watched Naomi clasp the woman's hands into her own and press them to her heart.

As reserved as Naomi was, this just proved how concerned she had been. Cheryl breathed a small sigh of relief. At least there wasn't anything wrong with Rebekah or her baby, though the farm, she wasn't so sure about.

The Yoders' barn looked as if it had been chopped in half. The side that was still standing leaned a bit. Cheryl grew nervous just looking at it. Someone, most likely the construction crew, had braced it up with poles and rope, but Cheryl wasn't certain those measures would be enough to keep it upright if a strong wind blew through. The other side had been leveled, the debris tossed into a Big Green container. The field where it stood was a complete mess. Mud caked everything around it from the men's boots to the caterpillar tracks on the big yellow equipment. In the middle of the field, a spout of water bubbled up like a mountain spring. A couple of the hard-hat men worked to stop the gurgle, completely ignoring the fray around them.

Cheryl sidled up to the nearest person. "What happened here?"

The Amish man grinned, though the action didn't reach his hard green eyes. "Someone's stealing old Yoder's milk."

His milk? Cheryl allowed her gaze to wander around the farm once more. "And that's why they have the bulldozers out here?"

The man shook his head. He looked to be about the same age as "old Yoder," and she noticed that his straw hat had a hole in one side. He wore the standard blue shirt and black pants, and like most of the Plain men standing around, his boots had seen more than their fair share of dirt. "Some of that is on account of the manure. *Ja*, Albert has a mess on his hands." He gave a small chuckle.

"Manure?" She turned to him, but he had already walked away. As she watched, he hobbled across the road and to the farm on the other side. It looked about the same as the Yoder place—a rambling white-frame house with a barn and a silo off to one side.

Although this man's barn was complete, and there were no bubbling streams chugging up from busted water pipes.

Cheryl watched him go. For the most part, the residents of Sugarcreek, both Amish and English, were the nicest people she'd ever want to meet. But there were some...

This man—Chupp if the name on the mailbox was correct, and she had no reason to believe otherwise—seemed to take great pleasure in the fact that his neighbor was having problems.

With a shake of her head, she looked back at the fray of people and vehicles but couldn't see Naomi or Rebekah Yoder any longer.

Chupp's words had piqued her interest. How exactly did one steal milk? Only one way to find that out, she thought, and eased her way closer to Chief Twitchell.

"If the milk has been disappearin' for months, why haven't you called me before?" the chief asked. Cheryl resisted the urge to lean in closer so she could hear them better, but Albert Yoder was angry enough that his voice was far from soft.

"You know how young people are these days." Albert shook his head. "They are too busy to do the job right. Used to be just the *Englisch* kids. Now it is all of them. I just figured they did not get all the cows in the barn. Or maybe they just missed the milking altogether. But I was with them last night, every step of the way. Then, come this morning, the tank was only half full—and after I did the morning milking too."

The chief made a couple more notes in his little pad then trained his gaze on Albert. Cheryl stayed well enough behind him so she was out of his line of sight. He would surely tell her to move along if he knew she was listening in. But there was something odd about the situation. Or maybe it was all the other chaos at the farm. The half-torn-down barn and the earth-moving equipment. Even the muddy field. It had recently rained, leaving soggy earth in its wake. And the temperatures had turned cool for July, leaving the moisture in place for a lot longer than normal. But that still didn't account for the growing pond off to one side of the barn.

"What about a leak?" the chief asked. He pointed to the water-logged ground.

"There is no leak in the milk vat," Albert said emphatically. "The water came from a busted pipe. These guys hit a water pipe trying to level the ground. Folks just don't do a job like they used to." He shook his head.

"And you think that excuses the sellin' of illegal raw milk?"

"I did not do anything wrong."

"That's not mine to decide, Albert."

"I thought a man had a right to defend himself in this country," Albert said. "You come out here saying I have been selling raw milk, and I tell you someone has been stealing it."

The chief stiffened, and Cheryl had a feeling he was resisting the urge to pinch the bridge of his nose. She couldn't say she blamed him. Sometimes talking with the Amish was like speaking English in a foreign land. The less dealings an Amish person had with the English, the harder it was for them to communicate with each other.

Whatever had happened, Albert Yoder clearly didn't understand.

The chief pulled a pair of handcuffs from the back of his belt and held them in front of him. "Now, Albert, I don't want any trouble."

Albert Yoder's eyes grew wide as he stared at the metal bracelets.

"I don't want any trouble," the chief repeated. "But I gotta take you in. I've got witnesses and a warrant."

"But...," Albert started, but his words stopped dead as the handcuffs clicked into place on his wrist. To the chief's credit, he didn't handcuff Albert with his hands behind him. Instead he allowed them to remain in front.

Off to the side, even amid the fray of noise and activity, Cheryl heard someone draw a sharp breath. She turned as Rebekah Yoder came waddling toward her husband.

"Be strong, Wife," Albert said with a quick nod. Unlike English couples who would embrace and perhaps kiss before one was led away, they just stared at each other, somehow relaying information that only the two of them knew with just their gaze. It was special and unnerving, all at the same time. Then the connection was broken as the chief steered Albert Yoder toward the back door of his car.

Cheryl felt rather than saw Naomi come up beside her. And together they watched as the chief came around to his side of the car, started the engine, and backed out of the drive. One by one, spectators dispersed. The police left, the firemen left, and the construction workers went back to work. What had been a near circus of activity slowed until only the few of them remained: Naomi, Cheryl, Rebekah Yoder, and the passel of kids that belonged to her and Albert. Everyone just stood and watched as if somehow the chief was going to bring Albert back and say that it was all just a bad joke.

"I don't understand," Cheryl said. She let her gaze drift between Naomi and Rebekah. Surely whatever happened would have to be very serious for the chief to take Albert away so close to the time for his child to be born. True that the Amish weren't quite as narcissistic when it came to childbirth and their children, but they were human beings. It was obvious that Albert cared for his wife very much. And though Cheryl herself had never experienced it, she knew that labor had to be a traumatic experience. She could only hope that Albert would be out of jail in time to see his baby come into the world.

A NOTE FROM THE EDITORS

We hope you enjoyed *Sugarcreek Amish Mysteries*, published by the Books and Inspirational Media Division of Guideposts, a nonprofit organization that touches millions of lives every day through products and services that inspire, encourage, help you grow in your faith, and celebrate God's love.

Thank you for making a difference with your purchase of this book, which helps fund our many outreach programs to military personnel, prisons, hospitals, nursing homes, and educational institutions.

We also create many useful and uplifting online resources. Visit Guideposts.org to read true stories of hope and inspiration, access OurPrayer network, sign up for free newsletters, download free e-books, join our Facebook community, and follow our stimulating blogs.

To learn about other Guideposts publications, including the best-selling devotional *Daily Guideposts*, go to Guideposts.org/Shop, call (800) 932-2145, or write to Guideposts, PO Box 5815, Harlan, Iowa 51593.

Sign up for the
Guideposts Fiction Newsletter
and stay up-to-date on
the books you love!

You'll get sneak peeks of new releases, recommendations from other Guideposts readers, and special offers just for you . . .

and it's FREE!

Just go to Guideposts.org/Newsletters
today to sign up.

Guideposts.

**Visit Guideposts.org/Shop
or call (800) 932-2145**

Find more inspiring fiction in these best-loved Guideposts series!

Mysteries of Martha's Vineyard

Come to the shores of this quaint and historic island and dig into a cozy mystery. When a recent widow inherits a lighthouse just off the coast of Massachusetts, she finds exciting adventures, new friends, and renewed hope.

Tearoom Mysteries

Mix one stately Victorian home, a charming lakeside town in Maine, and two adventurous cousins with a passion for tea and hospitality. Add a large scoop of intriguing mystery and sprinkle generously with faith, family, and friends, and you have the recipe for Tearoom Mysteries.

Sugarcreek Amish Mysteries

Be intrigued by the suspense and joyful "aha!" moments in these delightful stories. Each book in the series brings together two women of vastly different backgrounds and traditions, who realize there's much more to the "simple life" than meets the eye.

Mysteries of Silver Peak

Escape to the historic mining town of Silver Peak, Colorado, and discover how one woman's love of antiques helps her solve mysteries buried deep in the town's checkered past.

Patchwork Mysteries

Discover that life's little mysteries often have a common thread in a series where every novel contains an intriguing whodunit centered around a quilt located in a beautiful New England town.

**To learn more about these books,
visit Guideposts.org/Shop**